Chasing a Gem

Wendy Coffman

Contents

Chapter 1

"Never underestimate the power of colors."

Nan was a fanatic about color choices. She believed colors could improve your mood, spice up your personality, alter your behavior, you name it. The right colors could make or break an outfit, a painting, or a room. For all I knew, she thought the right color combination could get you elected President. Me, I go for the dark colors, the ones that slim you down, not make you stand out in a crowd.

She liked to reminisce about her days as a consultant with Color Me Beautiful, where she helped women find their color season based on their personality type. This was the genesis of the Sisterhood, her network of girlfriends who knew how to take care of themselves and take care of each other. All while looking fabulous in their color coordinated wardrobes.

This was long before I came along, the granddaughter who insisted that a gray tunic and black yoga pants was color enough. "I think my color season might be the dead of February in New Jersey," I once suggested. Nan would hear nothing of it, and tossed me a scarf full of reds, oranges, and yellows. And damn if she wasn't right. It looked amazing.

I think about Nan's love of colors as I am standing in Fiestaware up to my ears. And when I say my ears, I say this literally. I have two full sets of floor-to-ceiling shelving devoted to nothing but Fiestaware. Nan couldn't say no to an antique dealer with a pristine set of Fiesta's plates, saucers, and cereal bowls, their deep saturated colors seeming to call out her name. But the problem is, I say to Nan up in heaven, no one buys it anymore, no matter how awesome the colors are. There's simply too much of it available on the market. It's been four years since Nan died and the Fiestaware is not moving.

In case you're not familiar with it, Fiestaware is heavy as lead. You need some serious muscle to load a stack of these plates into your kitchen cabinet. And me, I'd need to be the Bionic Woman if I expect to rearrange the shelf-loads I've got here in the store.

I've tried organizing it by the colors of the rainbow. And believe me, I've got the dishes in ROY-G-BIV and then some. I've tried spacing them out strategically throughout the store. I've tried the fire sale approach. I've tried my best lighting. And I've tried eBay, of course. At this point, any good businessperson would tell me the dinnerware is costing me money, taking up too much space in the store. But my heart can't quite let go of Nan's favorites. Not yet anyway.

"Don't you know Fiestaware is radioactive?" That's Felicity, my best friend dropping in for lunch with two egg and cheese sandwiches from the corner deli. Both for me.

She's not joking. Fiestaware's red glaze was made with uranium until 1972. If you don't believe me, look it up. For a brief spell, there was a ban on this practice in 1943 when the uranium was needed to make bombs in order to kill people more quickly. But as soon as the war ended, they started right up again with the red radioactive ceramic glaze. Perfect for the slow kill.

"Care for a bowl for your salad?" I say, gesturing toward the wall of multi-hued ceramic ware.

Felicity and I step over to the alcove near the register so I can see if any customers are coming. Not today. It's the week after Christmas, and everyone is on retail overload.

"You busy or slow today?" I ask. Believe it or not, the week after Christmas can be one of the busiest weeks in a jewelry store, due to all the exchanges. I've known Felicity long enough to have learned this little-known factoid.

"A couple returns, a lot of re-sizing. One woman was clearly pissed off that her husband bought her this aquamarine ring, because it didn't exactly match her eyes. This ring was gorgeous. The husband wasn't half bad either. And honestly, does aquamarine really match anyone's eyes?"

"Bradley Cooper's?"

"Aw come on, Gracie, you still into that old guy?"

"Zac Efron?" I try.

"Too unstable!"

I can't keep up with all the stars like Felicity does. And she is a sucker for the blue-eyed ones.

"Chris Hemsworth," she says with authority. "The eyes, the shoulders...oh, and did I mention his Australian accent?"

Felicity digs into her Caesar salad with a relish that I reserve for a fine steak. Not that a fine steak is anywhere in my foreseeable future. I wish I could enjoy a salad the way she does. But to me, it's rabbit food. Two egg and cheese sandwiches – now that hits the sweet spot of cheap, fast, and delicious. Some days I even splurge and order it on a toasted bagel.

"You make any more progress on your mom's boxes?" Felicity asks.

My mother passed away this past August. Don't get too heartbroken for me. We weren't exactly close. But she'd left me everything she owned – a treasure trove of vintage fashions, costumes from her acting days, unique jewelry, and stylish household items. It was almost like inheriting a whole new antique store.

"I'll look through the boxes again. Maybe I can find some more of her fine jewels," I say, with an air of pretension, not honestly expecting to find anything valuable.

"That'd be terrific. My credit card is about ready to implode," she says.

Felicity repairs jewelry on the side. The job at the jewelry store barely makes her rent, and I know she spent a lot on Christmas this year. The combination of Felicity and a credit card is a dangerous thing. So I throw jewelry repairs and jewelry cleaning her way whenever I have the chance to give her a little extra spending money.

"You ever wonder what it would be like to be bionic?" I say to Fee, as I crush up the foil from my sandwiches.

"Bionic? What like a robot or something?" Fee asks.

"Extra strong, you know, like the Bionic Woman."

"Who's she? One of your superheroes?"

"One of my nerdy old TV shows. After an accident her legs and arm were replaced with super strong bionic parts. Her ear too. She could run, like sixty miles an hour to catch all the bad guys."

"That's what cars are for," Fee says. "I'll keep my own two legs, thank you very much," she continues, shooting down my temporary fantasy of being the next Jamie Sommers.

"There was a Bionic Man show too. Steve Austin. Totally crush-worthy," I go on.

"Now you're talking. I can think of a bionic part I

might like my man to have," Fee says. "And it wouldn't be his ear, if you know what I'm saying."

I laugh. Fee loves her innuendos.

We both look up as an elderly woman and her elderly daughter are trying to get in the front door. It sticks a little, and they can't get it to open. I can see them peering into the store, their squinted eyes disappearing into the lines of their faces. I rush over to let them in, which is our cue to end our lunch. I pop a piece of winter fresh gum into my mouth, Felicity slips out, and I face another afternoon in the shop, daydreaming of superpowers and blue-eyed actors.

The two women amble slowly through the store, talking in low whispers, and mercifully do not take it upon themselves to rearrange the displays I've worked on. You wouldn't believe how many shoppers like to rearrange items on my shelves. And when I say rearrange, I mean rearrange. One woman last week must have decided she needed one more ornament on her tree three days before Christmas. Our stock of ornaments was running low, as Christmas was just a few days away, and she proceeded to gather all the ornaments from each vendor and hang them on our tree in the center of the store, step back and determine which would look best on her tree. She spent all of twelve dollars to purchase one – a small German glass ball, red with a gold band across the center – and left the rest of the ornaments hanging on the tree where she'd seen fit to put them. What's disturbing is that I didn't find this to be unusual customer behavior at all.

Next through the door are two older gentlemen, and I say gentlemen because they are both sporting well-cut suits. If any men visit the store at all, they are more often than not dressed in their best retiree activewear. One of the gentlemen tells me they are looking for gifts for their wives. This sounds a little strange since the holidays just ended, but it strikes me as sweet just the same. They've got charming British accents, which of course endears them to me instantly. Who doesn't love a British accent? They pore over my jewelry cabinets and every basket of costume jewelry on the countertops.

"Have you got any fine jewels, say locked up for safe keeping somewhere reserved for your first-rate customers?" says the taller of the two. He stares at me for a beat too long, and it seems as if he's going to say something else.

"Now Jeremy, come now, that's insinuating that these jewels here aren't fine enough," says the other, with a small chuckle. "Don't want to offend the lovely lady before even making her acquaintance. And quite lovely she is." Both of them are clearly trying to charm me over, and who am I to turn down some charm? Even if it has to come from two elderly married men.

"No offense taken," I say. "I'm Grace, and it's a pleasure to have you in the store." I point them to my locked display cases with a small menagerie of jewelry that Felicity has told me might actually have some value, if I were ambitious enough to post each piece individually online. The one end of the display case is a collection of pieces with precious gems set in them, like rubies, emeralds, diamonds, but the gems are small and flawed, and not all that valuable. On the other side of the case are my semi-precious stones. Some of these can run a little larger, like the peridot, jade, and amethyst pieces that I've put front and center, but they still aren't going to make me a rich woman.

"What she really has her heart set on is sapphire. A

sapphire brooch or necklace, something that looks quite royal," Jeremy says. "She fancies herself a distant relative of the Queen."

I swear, it feels like I'm on the set of Downton Abbey.

"She does realize you shall never retire if she has a taste for sapphires," the other man says.

"I think that may be her plan exactly," Jeremy says, chuckling in a way I would imagine a footman or a valet might chuckle if the master of the house told a bad joke.

I open the case for them to have a closer look. "I've got some imitation sapphire, but nothing authentic at the moment. This ring here is my best imitation sapphire. The glass almost mimics the clarity and color of a real sapphire. But beyond that, you could try the jewelry store across the street."

"New jewelry is for the young. My wife, she likes the old world charm of an antique piece that has the mark of history in it. Surely you have something she would adore. The ring is lovely. Please show us your other sapphire imitations too. A fake sure would be easier on the wallet," Jeremy chuckles again.

They continue looking at the jewelry cases and begin peppering me with questions. Do I see a lot of sapphire coming in from the dealers? Have I sold much sapphire jewelry of late? I begin to think they are online sellers putting on a sadly transparent act. Online sellers will comb through antique shops to look for merchandise that is undervalued. They'll purchase it and then resell it at a higher price. They are reviled by most shop owners and often asked to leave if the shop owner gets wise to them. I don't let it bother me. Whether online or not, reselling is a practice as old as time. Kind of like these guys. As old as time.

"Can I give you my number, should you come across something suitable? My wife adores big, bold statements. Never one to be a wallflower," Jeremy says, handing me a post-it note with a number scrawled on it.

I suspect they think I don't know much about jewelry. The thing about sapphires is that it's hard to tell the difference between real sapphires and the synthetic kind that can be produced in a lab. They are hoping I'm undervaluing a real sapphire, accidentally selling it as synthetic.

His friend purchases a few used cookbooks on his way out. He absentmindedly hands me his credit card while he espouses that cooking for your wife is far more appreciated than purchasing jewelry for her. "No diamond is more precious than a person's time," he says, "which is why I am learning to cook. To give my wife time away from the kitchen."

Cooking versus jewelry. Which would you take? This seems to underline the difference between me and Fee. Fee? She'd take the jewelry guy for a husband over the cooking guy in a heartbeat. She barely even eats food anyway. Me, on the other hand, I would go for a guy who knows his way around the kitchen. Jewels are pretty, but don't do much for the soul. Good food, now there's something that can warm you through to the core.

As soon as this thought crosses my mind, a wave of depression hits me that I am actually talking about either of these geezers in a marriage context. Has it really gotten that barren? I think I know the answer to that.

And yet.

No sooner have the two gentlemen left, when the hottest man I have ever seen walks through the door. And when I say hottest, I do not say this literally. He is not the hottest man I have ever seen, but he is hands down the hottest man I have ever seen in *Antique Junction & Etc.* He is also quite possibly the *only man* under the age of 50 who has ever set foot in the door.

"May I, uh, can I help you?" I stammer, hoping my winter fresh gum has done its job.

"Just browsing," he says. I hurriedly clean up the remnants of my lunch, carefully hiding my greasy sandwich wrappers under Felicity's salad container in the trash can, trying to create the visual impression of having eaten the salad myself. I have no shame in taking credit where no credit was due. I only hope the place doesn't smell of eggs.

A trio of middle-aged women stops in next, one of them looking for a small milk glass container to hold her eyeliner and mascara. I show her to a few different options, including a jade-colored dish that I'm surprised hasn't sold yet. She goes for a white crimped hobnail vase, and as I'm wrapping it up for her, I see Mr. Handsome walk right out the door. It all happened so fast, that I wondered if he was an apparition.

"Did you just see that man?" I ask the women.

"The handsome one?" the middle woman asks with a smile.

"More like radioactive," her younger friend says.

"Just wanted to be sure I wasn't hallucinating," I say, thinking I prefer the hot guy's radioactivity over the Fiestaware's any day. As they take their receipts, they look at me with a mixture of amusement and pity.

Chapter 2

"Don't be fooled. Beauty is only lacquer deep."

Nan left a whole wall full of sticky notes with her home-grown aphorisms, born out from over thirty years of running Antique Junction & Etc. And if there's one aphorism she drilled into her only granddaughter's psyche, it was this one. *I have learned not to trust a single piece of furniture that comes into the store, no matter how nicely lacquered or how pristine it appears on the outside. Nan taught me the top-to-bottom inspection to ascertain whether a piece was handcrafted. I knew to look for the dovetails in the drawers, the hardware holding the handles in place, and the telltale signs of any replacement pieces or repairs.*

Me? If I were going to buy an antique dresser – which I honestly wouldn't do, but that's another story – I would gravitate toward the pieces that aren't refinished at all. I like to see the cracks in the original varnish. They remind me of alligator skin, and I love to rub my fingers over the crackly veneer and follow the lines like a maze across the surface. I figure, if you want to own an antique, it may as well look old, right? Too much lacquer can take away some of the original beauty, if you ask me.

I'm thinking about beauty right now. But I could care less about how deep it is, because what am I doing? I am talking to Felicity about Mr. Handsome. Again. It's New

Year's Eve, and I have been talking about him all week. Both Felicity and I are single again and there is no other man on the horizon for either of us to talk about. My brief 5-minute sighting of Mr. Handsome has sustained us for a full three days. All I know about him is that (a) he is a human being and (b) he is attractive. That seems to be as deep as we need to go at the moment.

"I think the bartender is flirting with us," Felicity says with a look of mischievousness.

"Of course he's flirting with us, Fee, that's his job!"

"Oh, right" she says, and takes another sip of her passionfruit martini. I myself stay away from the trendy cocktails. Call me thrifty, but I just can't manage a four-teen-dollar drink on the type of salary I pull from the antique store. I don't know how much Fee makes at the jewelry shop, but apparently it's enough to be ordering another martini already.

"And anyway, I thought you'd sworn off men until the new year," I say, looking at my phone for the time. "You've got twenty more minutes that you've promised to stay single."

"That guy across the bar is kinda cute," she says. Her eyes quickly develop a twinkle that she seems to be able to turn on and off at will. It's hard not to feel dull when sitting next to someone who shines like Felicity does.

"You can't ask him out 'til midnight. You made me promise to help you to stick to your pledge," I say.

Earlier in the year, Felicity had been dating Justin, a man she met on Cupid. They were together for over six months, which both of us had considered an unbridled success, when she learned he had purchased a diamond studded bracelet on Amazon. Amazon! And if this wasn't enough of an insult to her profession, she soon learned that the bracelet was not a gift for her, but rather a different woman he was seeing named Danielle.

"Polyamorous my ass," Felicity had concluded, and declared herself celibate for the remainder of the year.

The bartender tops up my ginger ale – it's my year to drive – and adds a perfectly-shaped maraschino cherry from the bar fruit bin. And if my eyes aren't fooling me, he even winks when he pushes the glass toward me. I appreciate the gesture, but I know he's just doing it for the tip.

"See what I mean?" Felicity says. "He's definitely flirting. Now I dare you to do an Audrey Horne with that cherry."

"Wha--?"

"Audrey Horne – an old Twin Peaks episode, c'mon get with the program!" And Felicity proceeds to steal the maraschino cherry and enact an unspeakable familiarity with it, all the while staring at the bartender, who thankfully is busy serving other customers.

"You're drunk my friend," I say, but can't stop myself laughing. Felicity is the least self-conscious person I know, and I love her for it. "And you'd better hope that doesn't go viral," I say, nodding at the attractive man across the bar who seems to have filmed Felicity's little act.

By this point, small plastic glasses of champagne are being handed out, courtesy of the bar owner, and the television is tuned to Times Square. The big moment is coming, our glasses are raised, but before I can throw my arm around Felicity in celebration, the man across the bar has appeared in between us, and has planted a New Year's kiss right on her lips.

I look to the bartender, in hopes of at least a New

Year's wink, but he is seriously engaged in French kissing the waiter. I raise my glass of ginger ale in the direction of absolutely no one, tilt my glass back for one final swallow, and feel an unpleasant splash as a hunk of ice slides down my glass into my teeth, spilling a few sad drops on my sequined blouse.

Looks like another night with just me and Spike.

Chapter 3

"It's not that I'm a Luddite. The old things were just better!"

*N*an had a disdain for all things new, which is why running an antique shop was perfect for her. She went to the grave insisting that her corded telephone was superior to any mobile phone. *"Give me one good reason I should trust a phone that's smarter than me,"* she once said.

Me? I'll take the new. While I like the charming and eclectic nature of the store, I put all that behind me when I leave work. I'll choose the new shiny stuff any day of the week. A new jacket every season? Sign me up. A new pair of shoes every month? Pinch me, I'm dreaming. A new car? I don't even know what a new car smells like, but I can guarantee you I'd like it if I could afford it.

And right now, in afterhours when New Year's Eve is blending into New Year's Day, I am ready to put the old year in the trash heap and start something new. I hope Spike is awake as I turn the key. I am certain he must have heard me ascending the stairs. My apartment is on the second floor of *Antique Junction & Etc.*, so I come up to visit him multiple times during the workday, and he's always there at the door waiting for me.

But not tonight. Tonight he's curled up in his bedding,

fast asleep, twitching like the bundle of nerves he is. I deliberately make a lot of noise and commotion as I add some lettuce to his food bowl, but he still doesn't wake.

Despite his obliviousness to New Year's Eve, I have to say that you really couldn't ask for a better pet than Spike. He's all the best cuddly parts of having a cat, but without the attitude and without the claws. He's litter trained and quite possibly the smartest and cutest lagomorph I have ever laid eyes on.

"Happy New Year, Spike," I say quietly. "Maybe this year will be our year."

As I'm finally drifting off to sleep Spike wakes up with a burst of activity. I hear him running, jumping, and sniffing around my room. And I can't help smiling when he decides to snuggle down next to me to continue his sweet little rabbit dreams.

∞∞∞

I decide to start off the new year right by lacing up my running shoes and getting some exercise. This assumes I can find my running shoes, which I do, after about an hour of digging around in my spare bedroom, which is a maze of my own belongings alongside the array of boxes and bags I cleared out of my mother's house after she passed. I find my shoes in the same place I left them last New Year's Day, only this year, one of the laces is gnawed off, courtesy of Spike.

Relaced and ready to go, I step out into the January morning, the sun glaring blindingly off the front display window of *Antique Junction & Etc.* The sun is like a laser beam hitting my eyes, coming in at the perfect angle to blind me no matter how I tilt my head. So I round the corner into the shade, only to find the wind is more punishing than the sun. One arctic blast stops my breath short, and I slow to a walk, which, in my opinion, is more in line with what the human body is meant to do. But it is far too cold to be walking without a heavy winter coat, so I settle for a slow jog. As I round the final corner of my one-square-block route, I see a man looking in the display window. It's him, Mr. Handsome. Gray overcoat, hands in pockets, a knit hat. The sunlight catches his breath as he exhales, creating a mystical steam around him.

My eyes are tearing up in the cold, my nose has started to drip, and frankly, my running tights are even tighter than they were last year when I ran on New Year's Day. And that's not a good sign. But I am trapped. I don't want to be seen like this, but there's only one entrance to my apartment, and frankly, I am freezing and want to get in out of the cold.

If I ever inherited any acting genes from my mother, now is the time to find them. I make a big production of stopping my run. Cue in the heavy breathing for overexertion, wiping the nonexistent sweat from my hairline, putting my hands on my head in that recovery position that runners always strike. I hope I look like I've just run a marathon, or at least a mile.

"Happy New Year!" he says, with a big wave like we are long lost friends. He really is to die for. "Will you be open tomorrow?"

"Nine to five," I say cheerfully, trying to channel Felicity's easy-going nature.

"Brilliant," he says and smiles at me.

Pow, aquamarine eyes. And when I say aquamarine, I mean aquamarine. His eyes are an exact match with the gemstone.

I stare like a deer in headlights as he fiddles with his keys, turns away from me with a brief wave, and walks across the street to get in his car.

I am still frozen in place. Thinking about those eyes. They are not just any aquamarine. I am talking about the high-end aquamarine gemstones Felicity sells to desperate husbands. Perfect clarity, rich blue color. I can't wait to tell Felicity.

But Felicity isn't answering her texts. I towel myself off after my hardly-deserved shower and head to the kitchen. I try her again.

Me: R u still with bar guy?

Felicity: Y

Me: Are u hungover?

Felicity: Y – vomit emoji

Me: Was he a mistake?

Felicity: Y

Me: Sorry – sad face emoji

Felicity: Next year, you drink, I drive

Me: Need help with outfit for tomorrow!

Felicity: U can count on me. Takeout at 6?

Me: Roger that!

Felicity: Don't say Roger. That's his name. I think, anyway.

Chapter 4

"Cash, credit cards, and shameless flattery accepted."

*N*an liked this saying so much that she had it blown up into a large sign that hung underneath the register. As much as I like to honor her memory, this sign was the first thing to go when I took over the store. I mean, give a girl a little dignity! It's now hanging in Carla's coffee shop, a few blocks from my store. Carla, the lovable chronically sex-starved seventy-five-year-old barista and former best friend of Nan, flirts with every eligible or noneligible male who dares set foot inside the shop. If they don't pay up in flattery, she charges them double.

I have never been good at accepting flattery or compliments, but Felicity has been working on me. She's all about positivity and being *fabulous babes*, as she likes to call us, and thinks that we deserve any flattery we are lucky enough to get. She, of course, gets more than I do.

She lets herself in my apartment. She looks good. She always looks good with remarkably little effort. Between the two of us, I'm the one who looks like I have a hangover. But she's the one who still smells like a distillery.

"Pinky promise you won't let me do that again, Gracie," she says with a twinkle in her eye that says she'd do it again tonight if she could.

She's brought with her two bags from the nearby convenience store called Wawa. Yes, you heard me right, Wawa. Anyone with any Philly in their blood knows what Wawa is, and it's best not to ask any questions. I unwrap my hoagie – call it a sub at your own risk – while she peels the lid off a peach yogurt.

Felicity lives up to her name. Friendly to a fault. She's always ready for a night out or to come to the rescue of a friend in need, and in tonight's case, I need an emergency wardrobe consultation. She settles into my breakfast nook where we've shared many laughs, heartaches, pork lo meins, and bottles of wine.

I finish my hoagie as she is still tentatively spooning small bites of yogurt into her hungover self. She sets it aside, her stomach not yet ready for semi-solid foods.

We head down my short hallway, and she sees my bedroom is already littered with discarded outfits. I pull out what must be my tenth option.

"Nah," she says, "too sexy to wear to work."

I try again. I stumble as I'm pulling up a pair of black slacks and nearly knock over the lamp on my end table. Spike startles and scampers under the bed, where I hear him nibbling on something. He's always squirreling bits of food away under my bed. I try not to think about what is accumulating under there.

"How's this?"

"Nope, too job interview."

Next I put on a grey scoop neck sweater and my jeans with the embroidered flowers down the left leg. I swear they fit just two weeks ago. I feel like crying when the zipper won't go up.

"Grace, the back of the sweater is all bunched up in your waistband! No wonder the zipper won't go!" Felicity

19

laughs. She has a delightful laugh which lightens up the mood and makes me realize how silly I am to be stressing over an outfit.

Like I said, Felicity lives up to her name. *Intense happiness.* But me? Of my 206 bones, I can't name one that is graceful. It begs the question: Is it really ethical to name your newborn Grace before you know whether or not she will actually be graceful?

I close up the top button of my jeans, straighten out the sweater, and strike my best runway model pose for Felicity.

"That outfit rocks! But save it for a date night."

"How do I know if there ever will be a date night?"

"Positive thinking! It's all in how you project yourself. He's on your territory, so you're in the position of power. I call it the P-O-P. Project confidence, and he will be asking you out before you know it," she says. Like it's that simple. For her, it probably is. For me, not so much.

I look at my stack of discards, looming like a mountain on my bed. "If we don't find an outfit soon, it's back to yoga pants and a tunic," I warn her.

"You look amazing in yoga pants and a tunic. Just be you! But go for a tunic with a little color in it."

"Don't say it!" I warn.

"Never underestimate the power of colors!" we say in unison, bringing the spirit of Nan into the room for a moment.

"Seriously, Grace. Just add a dash of color, and he'll see how you can really sparkle when you want to. Here, try this one," she says. "It'll bring out those emerald highlights in your eyes." And sure enough, we've found the perfect look.

Chapter 5

"The secret to eternal life on earth? Plastics!"

N an had a problem with plastic. She wouldn't sell any plastic items herself, and even sneered if vendors' stands had too many plastic items. She felt that plastics were the turning point for quality craftsmanship. For this reason, I was the only kid who carried a metal water bottle to school. This was back before BPA became the poster child for bad carcinogens we love to ingest and $25 metal water bottles became a status symbol.

When I stayed with Nan, plastics were the enemy. She wrapped my sandwiches in wax paper, which inevitably meant jelly was going to leak into everything else in my lunch bag. She nearly disowned me when she found plastic mechanical pencils in my backpack. "A perfectly good wooden pencil has now been turned to plastic too?" she said.

She would have flipped if she had lived to see the holiday decorations I had purchased for the store in the years since her death. Synthetic garlands, a plastic snowman statue. Even the lights were oversized plastic bulbs, and the candles were all fake, fake, fake. But I loved to overdecorate for Christmas, turning the store into a veritable wonderland.

And the veritable wonderland is exactly what I am doing – or rather *undoing* – this day after New Year's day. Coiling up the lights, reboxing the artificial tree, storing the decorations in, yes, a *plastic* storage container. Undecorating the store from the Christmas frenzy is a bit of a downer, but not this year. Today I'm humming to myself. It's amazing what the prospect of a cute male customer has done for my mood.

In my four years of owning the store, and the untold number of years I spent working for my Nan before she died, I can count on one hand the number of attractive men who have walked into the store unaccompanied by a woman. Scratch that, I can count it on one finger. Mr. Handsome is the only one.

I rent out booth space in the back display room to seven male antique vendors, four of whom like to flirt with me when they bring in new merchandise. And of those four, three of them are married, and the other must be pushing 80 by now.

Don't get me wrong. I still flirt back, no matter how old, no matter how married. Felicity says it's important to keep your flirting muscles active, even if the flirtees are completely unsound or unavailable. I take her advice to heart when Jakob rings the buzzer. He's got a dolly loaded with a large box and needs me to open the double door.

"Morning, gorgeous," he says, backing his way into the store.

"New year, new me," I say with a smile. I see him struggling to open the box and hand him a boxcutter. He gives me a sideways glance as I slide open the blade.

"I'm nothing if not dangerous," I say. I know, lines like this are terrible. That's the beauty of practicing them on unavailable men.

Jakob is the only man with the distinction of being part of Nan's Sisterhood. He was the newest member, admitted years after the women had cemented their friendships, but simply too much of a gem to pass up, despite his gender. He was the big brother they never had, the perfect husband who existed only in storybooks, and the handyman always at the ready whose hard, calloused hands and massive six-foot-four frame belied his warm heart.

Jakob unboxes a stunning side table with inlaid stone in an English ivy design. The tabletop is elegant, but the table legs are too ornate for my taste. The bowed legs are what they call *cabriole,* and end in paw feet. A bit over the top if you ask me. I don't care for disembodied animal paws on my table legs. These appear to be lion paws, if I had to guess. The worst paw feet, in my humble opinion, is the furniture paws that look like eagles' talons.

Now don't get me wrong. I'm as much a Philadelphia Eagles fan as the next South Jersey girl who doesn't really know what "offsides kick" means but goes to sports bars on game day anyway. But eagles' talons are for catching prey, not furniture legs. Still, I think Jakob's table will sell. It's a nice piece.

"You've been batting a thousand, Jakob. Your Christmas village sets sold out completely by mid-December. And remember that armchair you sold in November, like two weeks after you brought it into the store? That was amazing. I think this piece is going to go fast too."

"Thanks, Grace. This baby has got stunner legs, don't she?"

"Gotta love her curves," I say, almost cringing at myself. I've got to do better than this if Mr. Handsome decides to show.

I go back to wrapping up the holiday ornaments that didn't sell and disassembling the six-foot high toy soldier that I'd hoped to sell this year, but must have misjudged. Nan always counseled me that if it doesn't sell one year, that doesn't mean it won't sell another. Trends come and go, and then come back again.

Nan knew the business better than I ever will, but she never got hip to the online antique trade. Her margins suffered as eBay blossomed, but she still kept the store alive through pure grit. Me? I've got the whole cyber world at my fingertips. The buying and selling opportunities are endless. I've made some mistakes in my four years running the store, but I'm learning. Some days I even think this place could be my actual career – not just my consolation prize after bottoming out as a writer in New York.

But whatever I do, I want to stay true to Nan's vision. This store was her life. And she would say, it was not just her life, but the lives of others too. She wanted each customer to come away feeling like they were part of a story. She wanted every shopper to experience a sliver of history when they walked through her aisles.

I hear the bell over the entrance ring its pleasant tinkling sound to announce a customer is arriving. My heart palpates the minute I see his wavy hair. In what I can only describe as a momentary blackout, I vanish from the front of the store and find myself hiding in the back room, in Geena's stall. Will I ever mature beyond my middle school years?

The sound of footsteps is coming, so to calm my nerves, I make myself busy arranging Geena's wares. Another member of the Sisterhood, Geena is a purveyor of everything kitsch from the 1970's. Her stand looks like the sunrise with yellows, reds, and oranges brightening up the store. Eight-track tapes? She's got 'em. Owl figurines, mushroom string-art, glitter gold roller skates. Macrame – it's everywhere. You can't look at her wares without smiling. It's like sunshine on a cloudy day, she always says. The footsteps have stopped.

"When it comes down to it, am I a Dukes of Hazzard guy or am I the Fonz? That's what I ask myself when it's time to pack my lunch," says a deep voice.

"I, myself, prefer my peanut butter and jelly to ride Charlies' Angels style," I say, straightening out Geena's wall of metal lunch boxes. I'm still too afraid to look him in the eyes. I know what those eyes did to me when I saw them yesterday.

"Honestly," he says, grabbing the Happy Days lunch box from the shelf, "did kids eat smaller lunches back then?" He opens the box and takes out the thermos from its metal clasp. "Was bread smaller? I can't see how a sandwich and a bag of potato chips would even fit in here, with or without the thermos."

His pointless banter is just what I need. I can do pointless banter. My heartbeat settles to the point where I can speak almost naturally. "It was the miracle of Wonder Bread," I explain. "Back in the 1970's, with the advent of Wonder Bread, a full-sized peanut butter and jelly sandwich could be squashed to the size of postage stamp with no apparent detriment to the taste or texture."

"I guess that about explains it," he says cheerfully, and I finally look at him. I wasn't wrong about his eyes. Definitely aquamarine.

"The sandwich would then be coupled with the state-of-the-art Pringles potato chips, chips which were uniquely stackable so as to require no air space in between them," I go on. I may be laying it on a little too thick.

"Are those even made of potatoes?" he asks.

"Beats me," I say. "So, how can I help you?" In my own dreams, I can think of many ways I would like to help him, but I am running a business after all, so I stick to the script.

"I wanted to have a look at your jewelry. Necklaces, brooches, that sort of thing," he says.

Shit, I almost say out loud. *Of course* he's shopping for jewelry. And that can mean only one thing: a girlfriend or wife. I show him the various vendors who display jewelry, and he looks through them slowly as I look at him slowly. Crew neck sweater, strong neck, solid shoulders. His hairline is a little ragged, just enough not to look too clean-cut, with a few small curls bending in under his ears. He's studying the jewelry intently.

He doesn't find anything of interest in the back room, so I take him to the jewelry cases in my main showroom. After my mom died, I had to bring up two more jewelry cases from the basement to display all her wares. She was a jewelry hoarder if I ever saw one. Between the glass display cases, the baskets of chunky costume jewelry, and the standing carousels, her jewelry dominates at least half if not more of my inventory. And there's still more in my apartment.

I hope he finds the right thing for his beautiful girlfriend, I say to myself, setting about to sulk for the rest of the day. I decide he's really not that handsome after all. Teeth a little crooked. Needs to do something about his bushy eyebrows. Not quite tall enough for me, if I'm wearing heels. Talks a little strangely.

A text chimes in. Felicity no doubt.

Felicity: Any sign of him?

Me: He's here RN!

Felicity: And... what are you doing on your phone?

Me: He's shopping for his girlfriend! Of course. <sad face emoji>

26

Felicity: Girlfriends are temporary. Work it, Gracie!

He's leaning over one of the jewelry cases that I keep locked. It's the one with the precious and semi-precious jewelry that we have secured over the years. Some of it is left over from the days when Nan owned the shop, and frankly, the styles are outdated. For some of the most dreadful pieces, I've hired Felicity to refashion the stone into a more contemporary setting. She's masterful at creating gorgeous jewelry. Her pieces sell like lightning.

"My mother, her birthday's coming up, she loves jewelry of any sort," he begins.

Jesus, Mary, and Joseph, he's shopping for his mother! Did I not say love at first sight? Did I not say he is the picture of perfection?

"She especially loves anything blue – matches her eyes. What are these blue stones here?" he asks.

I show him a blue topaz brooch. A gorgeous stone, but again, an outdated setting. I also have a blue diamond necklace, which is really blue zircon, but still very classy. And my mother loved sapphire, so I have a few of her synthetic sapphire pieces on display. Believe it or not, synthetic sapphire is still considered actual sapphire, because it is grown in a lab in the same way it would grow in nature. So it's still fairly expensive. He's looking at one of her synthetic sapphire necklaces now.

"That used to be my mother's," I explain, "She was a jewelry hound. She could look good in the cheapest of costume jewelry to the finest of diamonds. Most people would look gaudy in what she wore, but she got away with it. She's the type of person who would turn heads wherever she went," I say.

"I see her daughter takes after her," he says with a twinkle in his eye.

I go into a full body blush, starting from the feet and working its way up to my forehead. Okay, I admit that I brazenly set him up for this line. It's the kind of thing Felicity has taught me to do, and I know she would be proud of me. And it feels terrific that he took the bait.

Truth be told, I am not the type of person who turns people's heads. Mousy brown hair, hazel eyes, medium height, pathologically clumsy, and carrying a few extra pounds. Okay, maybe more than a few. Let's just say, I identify as curvy. Felicity is not completely against me calling myself curvy, but she trying to persuade me to re-align my identity to *sexy* instead. It's all about body positivity, she keeps telling me.

"Is all of this jewelry from your mother's collection?"

"Most of the nicer pieces, yes. The ones that look like they're from somebody's great-grandmother's jewelry box, well, they probably are."

"Sorry to hear about your mum," he says. I swear he says "mum" and not "mom." It's kind of cute in a way.

"Believe it or not, this wasn't her entire collection. I have one more display case lodged in the back of the basement that needs a good cleaning. I've been procrastinating with hauling it upstairs, but I think that should hold the rest of her colossal collection. She had two walk-in closets in her townhouse, one of them devoted solely to her jewelry!"

"Need a hand with bringing the case up?"

I can't believe it. He took the bait again. Never in my wildest passive aggressive dreams did I think he would offer to help me with the display case. He may be a living, breathing Prince Charming.

The stairs creak as I lead him down into the depths of *Antique Junction & Etc.* As much as I love the display rooms of the store, I love the basement even more. It may look like a heap of trash to some people, but to me, it's a room of possibility.

The bulk of the items are furniture in serious need of refinishing. They are beyond what I could pass off as shabby-chic. I would say they are about two stiff breezes from the landfill. I do some of the work myself, but contract most of it out to Esmerelda. Esmerelda is a childhood friend of Nan's and she misses her as much as I do. She just finished an oak washstand for me that had been through a flooded basement and years in a dry, hot attic. Now it looks good as new. I can't wait for her to work her magic on the writing desk and the three-drawer dresser.

I move a box of refinishing supplies out of the way, and I notice Mr. Handsome does not seem as impressed with the basement as I am. In fact, he's looking at horror at the area I affectionately call my own personal land of misfit toys.

"I sure wish I could unsee some of these dolls," he says, his voice weakening.

I grab an eyeless ceramic doll and put on my best evil doll voice, "My name is Talky Tina, and I don't think I like you."

"Wait, Twilight Zone? That's going way back. You really know Twilight Zone?"

"Not as well as Charlie's Angels," I concede.

Now he's looking me in the eye, and even in the dim light of the basement, the blues are luminescent.

"I'm Benjamin," he says, which comes out as a total non sequitur, but I find it endearing.

"Grace. Pleased to meet you," I say, extending the doll's hand to meet his, and he jumps back in mock terror and laughs. The doll's hand will have to do. There's no way I'm letting him find out how sweaty my palms are.

He faces his fears and wades past the doll corner to my storage area. "Now it's my turn to be afraid," I say. "Spider phobia." I dust off the display case as best as I can, but the cobwebs have clearly won. I've learned over the years that a good pair of work gloves can go a long way toward overcoming the spider heebie-jeebies, and we wrestle the cabinet out of the corner.

And if I don't say so myself, I think we make a good moving team. We carry the cabinet up the stairs like pros, not once hitting a wall or stumbling up a step. I seem to anticipate which way he will be moving, not unlike a ballroom dancer reads the man's cues. Which starts my mind drifting to how nice it would be to dance with him on our wedding night under the moonlit skies of June. *Stick with reality, Grace,* I tell my daydream and snap out of it quickly.

"Well, as my late grandma would say, you're a gem," I say. "Come back tomorrow and I'll have this all set up with the final installment of my mom's collection. Maybe you'll find the right thing for your, uh, mum."

"Did I really say mum?" he sighs, shaking his head, and I think I hear him mutter *shit* under his breath.

The doorbell jingles, and an ancient couple is walking in the door. And when I say walking, I do not say it literally. Shuffling might be a better term. They are both shuffling so determinedly that I am certain one of them is going to trip. My carpet has a few tears in it, and there is the usual hodgepodge of stools, tables, coat racks, and chairs that stick out into the aisles. They are headed toward an old-fashioned egg basket that one of my vendors has displayed on the floor. It's the perfect item to get caught in the old man's cane. I can see a lawsuit materializing with every step they take. I tear myself away from Benjamin and go assist them. The woman collects vintage salt and pepper shakers, and they are eyeing a male and female cardinal set. Of course I myself stumble on the torn carpet on my way over to the couple. Like I said, grace is my name, not my strong suit.

A few minutes later, Benjamin appears, touches my elbow lightly and says he'll catch me tomorrow. And with that, the aquamarine eyes are gone, and I am left with all things old. As I'm closing up and shifting the jewelry case into position for tomorrow, I notice someone has brushed the cobwebs off the display case and written "pleasure meeting you, grace" in the dust. I hold my elbow in the spot where he touched me, and my crush level rises to an 11.

Chapter 6

"The definition of family is all relative."

N an was a loyal family person when it came to me and Mom, but she never spoke of any other family members. She had left her family home to marry my grandfather at the age of 18 and never looked back, not even when my grandfather left her right after my mom was born. But that didn't mean she didn't have family. It was just a family on her own terms. Regular customers, vendors, her hairdresser, my fourth grade teacher, even the letter carrier were welcomed into her orbit and formed the madcap miscellany that she called her extended family. It's been four years since her death, may she rest in everlasting peace, and customers still come in with stories of Nan that I'd never heard before. Sometimes I have to fend off the ones who still want to pinch my cheeks like they did when I was growing up and tottering under Nan's elbow at every corner of the store.

It could be said that this dusty old antique shop is not the most thrilling place for a young woman in the prime of her life to build her career. That would not be incorrect. It has not escaped my notice that most of our merchandise comes from the homes of dead people. And it would be fair to say that my customer base is headed in that same direction in the near future. And me? I'm not getting any younger either. Some days it's hard to tell which is louder – the ticking of my biological clock or the swinging pendulum of the 19th century grandfather clock that Jakob is hoping to sell.

But Antique Junction & Etc. is in my blood. Growing up, it was my home away from home. Nan kept the store open 364 days a year and had only hired one staff member in all of her years running the place. I always knew where to find Nan, and the door was always open for me.

She let me play with the second-hand toys as much as I wanted while my mother was at work at the department store, and as I grew older, she set aside a roll-top desk for me to do my homework after school. In all the old things, there was always something new to look at, always someone new to walk in the door. This was the hub of my childhood.

This is where I learned how things worked – back when they worked mechanically without the aid of a microchip. I learned to recognize the difference between authentic and imitation. I learned to appreciate the beauty in simplicity. And I learned to embrace my found family. The vendors and regulars were like aunts and uncles to me, and I don't know how I would have grown up without them.

By the time I was in high school, I would go days on end before returning to my mom's apartment, only to find my mother had taken an acting job in New York and would be gone for weeks. Other times a new boyfriend would appear, wholly infatuated with my mother as usual, and would leave shortly after learning that her overweight daughter lived there too. She would try not to be resentful of me. She was not a bad mom. At worst, she was a little absent from my life, but so was I from hers. Is it okay to admit that we simply didn't click?

She loved the big city, the theater, fine restaurants, fine clothing, and jewelry. She looked visibly skeeved whenever she spent too much time at Antique Junction & Etc., like she'd *need to take a shower immediately upon returning home. The more our paths diverged, the more I gravitated towards Nan. It made all three of us feel guilty. Mom for not being a more attentive mom, me for not being a closer daughter, and Nan for stealing me from Mom.*

As I heat up my Lean Cuisine, Spike waddles over to my feet. I can tell he wants a snuggle, and who am I to turn down a snuggle? He sniffs my miniscule portion of pasta al fredo with more than his usual vigor, but is only interested in a sprig of parsley. He may be onto something. His breath is fresh, his cotton tail white, and his physique is in top-notch shape. Maybe I need a diet of parsley and lettuce too. I laugh to myself at the likelihood of that ever happening.

Just as I am wondering what the policy is on eating two Lean Cuisines for dinner, Felicity rings the buzzer. She's coming up to help me sort through the final lot of my mom's jewelry. But really what she wants is the low-down on Benjamin. I toss the Lean Cuisine back in the freezer and let my friend in.

Felicity's color has come back after a full day of abstinence, and she hunts through my fridge for something to eat. She manages an apple and a wedge of Skinny Laughing Cow cheese and calls it dinner.

"Don't overdo it," I say dryly.

"Oh, I had a big lunch, now let's hear about this guy! Ben's his name?"

I proceed to tell her the whole story, with as much juicy embellishment as I can manage. Moving the display case, dusting off the cobwebs, his arcane knowledge of the same 70's and 80's sit-coms that I watched time and again with Nan. Was there any doubt we were a match made in heaven?

To celebrate my good news in the male department, Felicity reaches into her handbag and pulls out a bag of Hershey kisses and the bottle of prosecco that we never got around to on New Year's Eve, thanks to Roger stealing my date.

We decide on *Avengers: End Game*, because Fee wants her fix of her blue-eyed beau Chris Hemsworth. But between her getting up every 5 minutes to refill her prosecco and me being distracted by the events of the day, neither one of us pays much attention.

Next Fee's phone is beeping roughly every 20 seconds. She's quickly deleting every text, and I begin to wonder who could be texting her that rapidly. I look over her shoulder and instantly wish I hadn't. Apparently, Roger has a penchant for anatomically explicit photographs that are intended for Fee's eyes only.

Fee just laughs. "See what I mean? The guy is eager, isn't he? But he's just not my type." She deletes a few more.

"Are you going to respond to him?"

"Not with a picture, if that's what you're asking!"

"Shouldn't you at least tell him you're not interested?"

So we sit down together and compose a Dear John text where I help Fee understand how to let someone down gently. Having been dumped more times than I can count, I feel I'm an authority on what the dumpee wants to hear.

"You've got to let him down gently, Fee. Allow him some dignity," I say.

"Dignity? After two dozen dick pics in a row?"

"Good point," I concede.

But still. Fee has only ever been the dumper. She just doesn't get it. When she hits send, I start to feel some sort of compassion for Roger on the receiving end of the text. Even though I've seen his face exactly once, in the brief moments before it was smashed up against Fee's mouth, I still feel for him. And now that I've seen his most private parts being unceremoniously deleted off of Felicity's iPhone into the trash heap of cyberspace forevermore, I really feel the guy's pain.

Roger may have turned out to be a dead end for Fee, but I know the next guy will be right around the corner for her.

Fee is tipsy from the prosecco as the movie winds down. She gives me a hug and a squeeze and I hold up Spike to let him give Fee a nibble and a sniff before she leaves.

"I feel something good about this guy Benjamin. Be yourself Grace, and I know something will work out," she slurs, putting her right arm into the left arm hole of her jacket.

I don't feel so sure myself. But a girl can hope, right?

Chapter 7

"Refinishing isn't just for antiques."

*N*an was into self-improvement before self-help books were even a thing. She figured if you could give an old dresser new life with a handheld sander and some stain, you could probably rejuvenate yourself too. And she didn't believe in quick fixes. She knew that any true change required hard work, and she trusted the old tried-and-true methods. Need to get smarter? Read the classics. Need to lose weight? Eat less! Need to be a better person? Get thy ass back to church. "Remember, we are all works in progress," she would tell me. "And a work in progress can always be improved and should never be taken lightly."

I spend the morning rearranging the front room to make space for the jewelry case. Arranging jewelry in a showcase is an art in and of itself, and Nan has taught me well. I replace the light bulbs in the lighted display case with softer lighting, and I elevate mom's best pieces, giving them center spots beneath the glass where there's little glare. I line up her rings by color and style, and match them with necklaces and earrings where I can. My mom, bless her soul, would approve, I know it.

My favorite piece of all is a blue-green tourmaline and diamond studded choker. I used to call it her turtle necklace when I was little because of the pendant's shape. I have put it in and taken it out of the display case a dozen times, not sure if I can part with it. I would never in a million years have an occasion to wear it, but all the same, I decide to keep it.

All of my vendors have been in the store today to collect receipts and square up their space rental. January and February are our slowest months, both in-store and online. But we all had a decent holiday season, so no one is complaining. Geena and Jakob are both overhauling their arrangements and moving out a few things that they've sold online.

I also meet with a contractor. After two strong years in a row and a small inheritance from my mom, I finally want to put a little money into the store and give it a refinishing of its own. We discuss plans, and he pulls up the corner of the wall-to-wall carpeting, which looks like it was stitched during the Johnson administration. A beautiful wood inlay is visible beneath the dust and the scratches, and he explains the process he's going to use while sanding the floors, but all I can envision, despite his promise that the sanding is dustless, is having to wash each and every item in the entire store, from the smallest thimble to the set of 4 intricately hand-carved chairs to the shelves upon shelves of knickknacks, to yes, the never-ending towers of Fiestaware. Yet still, I can't wait to get the renovation underway.

By three o'clock, my nerves are frayed. Every time the doorbells jingle, I tense up in anticipation of Benjamin coming, but by now I'm starting to think he won't show. Geena hoists her macrame handbag over her shoulder as she's headed out the door.

"There's a good-looking fellow out there. He's been peering in the window on and off all day. He must be freezing! I think he's waiting for us to clear out so he can see you alone," she says to me. She shouts out the door, "Come on in, I don't bite!" and lets Benjamin through the door. I can see Geena looking him up and down to make a 10-second assessment. She pantomimes the "call me" motion as she leaves. She'll want a full update too.

Benjamin looks like a scolded schoolboy as he squeezes past Geena. She can have that effect on people.

He is coming toward me, his nose and cheeks red from the cold. I hold up my finger and disappear for a few minutes, returning with two cups of hot chocolate with miniature marshmallows.

"Just what the doctor ordered," he smiles.

"Starsky and Hutch or Partridge Family, your pick," I say, holding both mugs out to him.

"Why do I sense I'm being judged? Hmm, I guess I can't go wrong with the Partridge Family."

"You do have a little David Cassidy in you. Ever consider growing out your hair?"

I watch him sip his hot chocolate, and immediately I can tell he's my type of guy. He's drinking around the mini marshmallows, saving them for last. Only a brute would eat the marshmallows first. His jawline, his lips, his hands grasping the mug. It's hard not to stare. Mesmerized by watching him, I take too big a sip, and of course I scald my lips and tongue. I'm trying not to show my pain when I feel his hand under my chin.

I freeze up, not sure what he's doing, and then, with the edge of his thumb, he carefully wipes away the melted marshmallow that had formed on my upper lip, smiling at me with a tender expression on his face. I love the smile lines around his eyes. In the movies, he might have let me lick his thumb seductively, or maybe he would have licked his own thumb seductively, and at the very least we would have ended up making out. But this isn't the movies. So I just smile back at him and he wipes his thumb on his jeans. Not exactly the movie scene I am dreaming of, but I'll take it all the same.

He whistles in approval as he sees the new jewelry display case. I show him two necklaces I think he might like for his mom. He studies the entire case and then asks about the aquamarine pendant necklace. It's lab created, not real, but still a nice piece. I don't recall my mother ever wearing it. Then again, there weren't enough days in the year to wear everything she had.

I try not to gawk, but as he bends over the case, perusing each piece, the scant light of the January day catches his hair, creating an aura behind him.

"This your mom's complete set?"

"The whole kit and kaboodle," I say, cringing at myself. Who says kit and kaboodle? I'm clearly spending way too much time around old people.

"You weren't kidding when you said she was a jewelry hound. It's hard to choose. Would you?— Aw, no, I can't ask you that."

"Ask me what?"

"I was going to ask if you would try on this necklace, so I could see how it looks on someone, but that sounds pretty creepy, you know?"

He looks so earnest and so *un*creepy when he says this that I just laugh.

"If I was wigged out by creepy, I wouldn't be working here," I say.

I open the case and remove the aquamarine pendant necklace. Not my color palette, as Nan would agree, but it is a beautifully designed necklace. I start to become self-conscious about modeling a necklace for this man

I barely know when, just in the nick of time, the spirit of Fee overcomes me. I think about her Audrey Horne impersonation with the cherry stem and try to channel her unique combination of sultry and nonchalance, as I don the necklace. I don't think I've mastered it, but as Fee reminds me, flirting takes practice, practice, practice. I position myself in that small stream of sunlight so that he can see the gem shining.

He looks at the necklace, and I lift my chin so he can see it better. I see the beginning of a smile around his lips, his eyes widening. He seems to have found the necklace he wants. I wonder if he can feel me sinking into the facets of his aquamarine eyes. I wonder if he knows how his half-smile has me melting behind the countertop. I wonder if he knows that I don't want him to go yet.

I go to unclasp the necklace only to find that I have clasped it over one of those fine curls at the back of my neck which insist on spiraling into a rat's nest on a moment's notice, which apparently was the moment I closed the clasp. I have my elbows up in the air trying to undo the necklace, and the more seconds that pass without success, I begin to worry if I might have sweat stains on my shirt or unsightly arm baggage that I don't want him to see. Things are rapidly spiraling in the wrong direction. The harder I work, the more tangled my hair becomes.

"A little help here?" I say.

Now it's his turn to laugh.

"May I?" he asks, as he walks behind the counter. I hold up my hair, and he stands behind me in what I can only describe as the best moment of my waking life up until now. If you didn't know I had just tangled my hair in a knot while trying to sell a used piece of jewelry, and if there weren't a cash register two feet away from us, and if we weren't in a small town in South Jersey whose best days were behind it, you would think we were two lovers sharing an intimate moment. Just picture this: the handsome man stands behind the loving woman, draping an expensive necklace upon her willing neck before taking her to a five-star restaurant on the Rue de Rivoli.

He smells of something sweet, maybe spices mixed with the cold winter air. He laughs nervously, and I pray to heaven above that I am not sweating, shaking, or exuding the smell of my pop tart breakfast. He proves too adept at untangling my hair, and the moment ends as quickly as it begins. Nevertheless, I think, between scalding my tongue on the hot chocolate and tangling my hair in the necklace, my clumsy self is doing me a solid today.

He returns to the customer side of the counter. "I'll take it, even though I am sure it looks better on you than it will on my mom," he says.

I'm wrapping the necklace and ringing him up at the register when he says quietly, almost to himself, "This is not what I expected."

"I'm sorry, you're not happy with the necklace?" I say.

"No, no, of course. The necklace is lovely. Just like the... hot chocolate," he says with a pause, eyes connecting with mine again, as he reaches out his hand for the package.

Cue the slow motion cameras. With the powers of perception that many single women develop with enough practice, my brain is able to view his outstretched hand in a split second and ascertain the following: Strong, defined, lightly calloused, clean, well-groomed. In the next split second: Optimum hair growth, suggesting evolution beyond the Neanderthal, but not so feminized that he'll be borrowing my hand cream. Conclusion? Perfect hands.

All I can think of is whether his perfect hand will touch mine. And it does, however briefly. I hope the lightning bolt of electricity that he transmits through my fingertip is reciprocated back at him. Does he feel it too?

A burning flush rises up in my face, and in my nervous self-consciousness that this is my last chance to see this man, I jam my index finger in the cash register drawer and let out a burst of profanity. Like I said, grace is not my strong suit. But please understand that cute guys shopping in antique stores and wiping marshmallow off my lips is not something that happens every day. You're gonna have to trust me on that.

Chapter 8

"Never trust a man with a flask."

N an didn't believe in hiding anything. She felt information should be open to all, and that true friends – and lovers – did not hide things from one another. And nothing symbolized this more than the flask, the ultimate tool for clandestine behaviors. "If a man has to hide his drink, that's a sign you need to run. Fast and far!" she would say.

Despite this, Nan was fascinated by our collection of antique flasks, and so was I. She loved the lore of prohibition and speakeasies and the clever workarounds people found to keep an underground economy going.

Me, I just thought the flasks looked cool. We had a colorful cloisonne hip flask in the store for years. It was too frilly for most customers' taste, hence the many years it remained in our collection, but as a little girl, I thought it was beautiful. It wasn't a true antique, like some of the Russian cloisonne hip flasks you can buy on auction, but this didn't matter to me.

When I was in second or third grade, I was repeatedly nagging Nan about whether I could use the flask. When she said no time and again, I saved up enough money to buy it from the store myself. I was so proud of my purchase, and it fit perfectly in my lunchbox. I couldn't wait to unscrew the lid in the cafeteria and sip down my apple juice in style.

This lasted about five minutes into the lunch period before I was quietly escorted to the office. I still remember the look of mortification on my mother's face when she entered the principal's office. But the look on Nan's face was something altogether different. If I had to guess, all these years later, I would guess she was doing all she could to hold back a laugh.

It's promising to be a quiet January weekend in the store, and Jakob has offered to run the place while I join Felicity for the annual jewelers' convention in Atlantic City. It's just an hour away, but we're doing it up Felicity style with the hotel room, a couple shows by has-been recording artists, and room service for breakfast, or so she promises me.

The convention is meant to unveil the new year's trends in fine jewelry, but truth be told, it's not a convention. It's jeweler party time, like spring break in Miami, a pub crawl on St. Patrick's day, New Year's Eve on Time's Square, Mardi Gras in the Big Easy. You get the idea. The Christmas rush behind them, these jewelers need to let off some steam.

What's more, every year the jeweler's convention coincides with Felicity's dream come true: a bodybuilder's convention. The two groups share the same convention center, coming together to produce one of the stranger party dynamics. Burnt-out jewelry bench-workers try out the newest dumbbells and exercise bands, while steroid-fueled bench-pressers wonder why the gold chains don't fit around their necks. Add enough alcohol to the mix, and things get interesting.

Last year the bacchanal atmosphere didn't have the best results for Felicity, so this year, I've come along. To babysit. Fee's two annual New Year's resolutions are to drink less and to vet the boyfriends more, two resolutions that can work in direct opposition to one another once one of them starts to slip. That's where the babysitting begins.

She's working at her store's booth on the convention floor. In addition to the store's pieces, her boss has let her display some of the jewelry that she designs herself. I think it's far better than the store's offering, and in my humble opinion, Fee could be making more profits for the store if her boss would just make her the lead purchaser. One day I know she's going to make it as a jeweler. Whether it's owning her own store or custom-designing for the stars, I don't know. But this woman has got a gift, and the world needs to know it.

We start the morning with a cup of coffee, and my job is to ensure that neither Felicity nor any of her jeweler friends allow the coffee to be spiked any earlier than eleven-thirty in the morning.

The convention floor looks like a mix of jewelers, shoppers, and fashion designers, all trying to out-style one another, as well as the bodybuilders wandering in from the convention next door, whose curiosity has got the better of them. I browse the booths, and I am stunned by the price tags. Within twenty minutes, I am convinced that I am in the wrong business. I am trying to squeeze every last penny of life out of a vintage new-in-box Barbie doll collection while the real money is happening in the sparkling minerals and precious stones that are dazzling the dollars right out of people's bank accounts.

Felicity excuses herself to go to the bathroom and I take over the booth. This worries me because (a) I'm leaving her out of my sight and (b) I don't know enough about her wares to put on the big sell. But we can't very well leave the booth unattended, so I allow it.

As I wait for her, sipping my coffee and enjoying the people-watching, I get the sense that I myself am being watched. Each time I turn my head, I have the distinct feeling that my watcher is vanishing, but yet, I can't catch sight of anyone. I can't decide it if is creepy or titillating, but in the spirit of positive thinking, I'll go with the latter.

Fee returns with, I kid you not, a silver flask under her palm.

"Vintage flasks are my department, Fee," I say, trying to take it from her.

"Isn't this adorable?" she says. "I never knew whiskey could be so cute."

"Where'd you get that?" I ask.

"Aidan," she says, as if I am supposed to know who Aidan is.

"Is he the weightlifter who wanted to sneak into the exhibit hall and do it with you on the gym equipment last year?" I ask, remembering vaguely that something bad happened.

"Ha, no, that was Eamon," Fee laughed. "I'll never forget the incident with the resistance bands," she says with a satisfied sigh.

"So who's Aidan?"

"He's this year's man," she says airily, as though she's already smitten.

"Okay, spill it, when did you meet him?"

"Outside the ladies' room. He's dreamy."

"And in five minutes' time, he handed you a flask of whiskey and asked you to go to bed with him?"

"More like seven."

"Seven what?"

"Seven minutes. It was probably seven minutes."

I don't doubt her. Her confidence with guys knows

no bounds. On the flip side, my babysitting skills clearly leave something to be desired.

"Well, you're not doing so bad yourself. I see that cute guy eyeing you," Fee says.

"Cute guys don't eye me," I say.

"Maybe they didn't eye the old Grace, but you better believe they eye the new Grace."

"What new Grace? What are you talking about?"

"You, Grace! Don't you see you're changing?"

"How so?" I say. I look at Felicity, and she's giving me her undivided attention. Just when you think she's shallow and flighty, she does this thing where she gives you her full attention and says something perceptive that cuts to the core.

"I think it has to do with your mom passing away," she begins. "I know you really miss her, so don't take this the wrong way. But ever since she passed, I think you've really blossomed."

"Hmm," is all I can muster.

"Your mom was always sweet to me, but I could see that she was very critical of you and your decisions. And you're a full grown adult! I can only imagine how that felt when you were a little girl. Now that you're able to just be yourself, I think your confidence is growing. And it shows."

I think about this for a few minutes, and while my first instinct is to defend my mother, I definitely see a grain of truth in what Fee is saying. Since my mother died, I have noticed a change. I am making decisions faster. Censoring myself less. Doubting myself less. Fee may be right. And it does feel freeing—all of which sends me down the guilt path, feeling like a bad daughter for not missing my mother more.

"So where is this cute guy who is allegedly eyeing me?" I say, not wanting to fall into a well of introspection.

"He's behind that mannequin now, by the booth with all the red velvet display boxes. See him?"

I look to the booth, and I see him at last. But my head won't process what in the world he might be doing at a jewelry convention in Atlantic City. All I can tell is that he is looking at me. And I'm sure he is the person who has been sneaking looks at me all morning. He waves a small wave toward me. Benjamin?

"Go, Grace. I promise I won't drink a lick of this whiskey until eleven-thirty, as scheduled."

"Breath mints!" I say, and I rummage through my handbag until an old roll of Breathsavers surfaces. The last thing I need is coffee breath.

"Now go!" Felicity says, nearly kicking me in the rear.

∞ ∞ ∞

"I thought that was you, Grace," Benjamin begins, as though it's the most natural thing to be seeing each other in this convention hall. He steps away from the booth where two saleswomen were showing him a diamond studded tennis bracelet, and walks me through the aisles toward a quieter spot.

His shoulders square off beneath his gingham shirt, and his neck muscles press against the collar as he turns to look at me, walking a few steps behind him. I try not to stare at him, but the way he moves is so fluid and confident that I can't help feeling drawn toward him. He motions for me to walk in front of him and guides me along with his hand lightly resting on my back. *Don't trip, don't stumble*, I will myself in my head. And it works, at least for the time being.

"You are looking lovely this morning," he says.

"That doesn't answer my question," I say.

"I don't recall you asking a question," he answers.

"When someone you just met two days ago shows up at a jewelry convention in a sad has-been casino hotel full of horny, desperate jewelers, the question should be obvious," I say.

"What question?" he asks innocently.

"What in the world are you doing here?

"Oh, that," he says.

"Are you following me?"

"The same could be asked of you," he says, turning toward me, touching my sleeve gently, and running his finger along the underside of my wrist.

"No, I'm not following you. I'm here babysitting," I say. His touch is lighting fires within me, and I fight to stay coherent.

"Last I heard they didn't let babies into the casino resorts," he says, his eyes growing a playful twinkle.

"I'm babysitting a full-grown friend so that she doesn't regret her very existence in the morning."

"Not the woman with her tongue in that fellow's ear, is it?"

A look of horror passes over my face at my utter failure to babysit Fee properly.

"Just a joke. Made you look though, right?"

"Ha ha," I say dryly. "You still haven't explained why you are here."

He looks down at his hands for a moment, as though considering his answer.

"For work," he says, simply enough.

His short answers are infuriating me, but he steps closer to me, and I feel the electricity again. With my wedge heels, we are standing eye to eye, and his focus zeroes in on me. The peripheries go blank – the voices, the people milling about, the overhead lights – and it's just the two of us for a moment or two.

"Work? What sort of work?" I say.

His cell phone rings and he looks distracted for a second while he declines the call.

"Can I tell you over dinner tonight?" he asks.

"Dinner?" I say, suddenly weak in the knees.

"Yes dinner. It's the meal after lunch. How about the sushi restaurant near your shop?"

"I'm staying here over tonight, you know, as the baby-sitter."

"Tomorrow, then?"

I start to nod, and then my cell phone starts beeping a series of rapid-fire notifications.

Felicity: Need you
Felicity: Now
Felicity: Please
Felicity: And sorry

I show Benjamin the phone, and he waves me away to go join my friend, with that same irresistible half-smile that makes it hard to tear myself away.

I weave through the exhibits and momentarily get disoriented, take a wrong turn, trip over a power cord, apologize profusely to the jeweler whose lightbox I just disconnected and whose Monster energy drink just spilled on the industrial carpeted floor, and finally make it to Felicity's exhibit. In front of her booth are two men, circling each other like prize fighters and about ready to duke it out. They are both extremely handsome and extremely wasted. At ten o'clock in the morning.

I take a deep breath, invoke the spirit of Nan and the fabulous women of the Sisterhood, and barge through, hoping not to get sucker punched in the process.

"Break it up, break it up guys!" I boom. Being of impressive stature can have its advantages, especially when breaking up drunks, although I must admit I have my work cut out for me, given that these particular drunks are built like brick shithouses. I put my arm around the taller of the two and walk him over toward the exit to the capable hands of a security guard. For someone who looks like the Incredible Hulk, he's actually fairly pliable when a strong woman tells him what to do.

"C'mon Eamonn, why'dja have to go and pick a fight?" Fee is pleading with the shorter guy when I return.

"Okay, okay, sorry love, I just wanted to be sure the guy was treating you right," Eamonn says.

"Let me guess, the tall guy was Aidan, the one who gave you the flask?" I say. I honestly don't even know how she keeps them straight from year to year.

"Yes, isn't he cute?" Fee says when Eamonn finally leaves.

Leave it to Fee to have two guys fighting over her. Tonight's going to be a long night.

∞∞∞

By some miracle from the great god above, Aidan and Eamonn both vanish from the convention, and Felicity and I are left to ourselves, much to her disappointment. We venture into the shopping strip and I spot a dim sum restaurant that does not serve alcohol. It's perfect. The hip flask notwithstanding, I believe my babysitting successes are beginning to stack up in my favor if I can just drag dinner out long enough to sober her up.

I finally tell her about my afternoon's events, and she is thrilled for me. She is the type of friend who can be as genuinely excited about my dates as she is about her own.

"I don't even know where he's picking me up! I was too nervous, and I seem to have typed in his cell number wrong, because when I texted it, I got back 'this is sexymama, who 'dis?'"

Felicity flags down a server for another pass at the shrimp balls. "Do shrimp even have balls?" she asks rhetorically.

I try picking up a shumai with my chopsticks, and through some act of physics, one of my chopsticks goes skidding across our table and lands on the floor. "Wherever he takes you, may I suggest you stick with a fork and knife?"

I make a mental note to practice with chopsticks for the sushi restaurant. It's a restaurant I've only tried once. The prices are special occasion only, which in my opinion, this is. I just haven't told Fee about the restaurant, because I want to keep some bits to myself. I love Fee like a sister, but if I tell her everything, it might become her date and not mine.

Fee's just about as alone as I am in this world, but you would never guess it for how outgoing she is. Her father skipped out on the family when Fee was a teenager, and her mother suffers from a series of mental health issues which make their relationship impossible to maintain. But she's the reason Fee stays in New Jersey, even though I know she's itching to get out. She visits her mom every

Sunday evening, which usually results in a screaming match or a silent treatment for the next week. Fee takes her to doctors' appointments, argues with her over taking her medications, and tries to get her out of the house every now and then. I think she does it partially out of obligation, and partially out of some deep-seated desire for approval in her mother's eyes.

Her older sister Suze stuck around until Fee finished high school and promptly left for New York. She hasn't looked back and doesn't feel any guilt over it. Where I failed in Manhattan, flashing my brand new MFA in creative writing and lasting less than a year as an entry level copywriter, Suze skipped the degree, taught herself graphic design, and succeeded to the point where she has to turn clients away. She sends her mother some money, and apart from that, thinks it's not her responsibility to take care of a woman who refuses to listen to her doctors.

A server comes by and refills our tea. I love to cradle the little teacup in my hands and smell the scent of the jasmine wafting up. And the feeling washes over me again that something good is coming my way this year.

"Ever hear any more from Roger, the guy from New Year's Eve?"

"Turns out his name was Robert, and yes, he called me."

"After the Dear John text you sent him?"

"Yes, he wants me to give him another chance."

"Naturally," I say. Who wouldn't fall for Fee?

"When his wife goes out of town again."

"Oh shit, it's even worse than you thought! Maybe I should have let you send the insensitive Dear John text after all."

"Exactly!" Fee sighs. "But we've got more important

fish to fry. We got to figure out what you're going to wear for your date tomorrow night!"

We agree it's time for the nuclear option: the scoop neck sweater and embroidered jeans.

Chapter 9

"A slow brew is the sure sign of sophistication."

A s you might guess, my Nan had no interest in the modern day coffee movement. She derided the enormous menus and the even more enormous coffee making stations at Starbucks. Worse yet was the Keurig machines, which, you and I both know, could brew a decent cup of coffee with zero effort whatsoever. But not so in her mind. "You want an espresso? I'll make you an espresso!" she'd say to a customer carrying around a Starbucks cup. She would grab her stovetop aluminum espresso maker circa 1910 and disappear into our kitchen area where we had, I kid you not, a plug-in hot plate that probably broke every fire code ever written. But I gotta tell you, her espresso tasted like you were drinking the coffee beans right off the tree. Never bitter, never weak, and always hot in a way that never cooled off, from the first sip to the last.

Showing off like this was also a surefire way to sell the stovetop espresso pots. Nan had collected a number of vintage espresso pots, including an assortment of Bialetti moka pots from her Italian friends and neighbors as they moved on to automatic drip pots or Keurig machines, both of which Nan considered nothing less than a sacrilege for a self-respecting Italian American. Every time she sold a customer one of the vintage espresso pots, I wondered if they actually learned to make espresso the old fashioned way, or just told the story of *the loony store owner who one day made them a free espresso on her hot plate.*

I'm a little ashamed to admit that I replaced the hot plate complete with its fraying cord and ungrounded plug with none other than a Keurig machine. I mean, give a modern girl a hand when it comes to the morning joe.

I'm cleaning off Nan's collection of elegant Italian espresso pots – which, admittedly, haven't sold as well since her death – when a customer begins asking me questions about how to use them. I know the basics of how to brew espresso and how the moka pots work, but I remember that Nan had written up a tip sheet that she kept in a file box full of index cards. She loved to organize her life with index cards.

I'm sorting through the file looking for the espresso-making notes when I come across a random index card, written in her handwriting. The top of the card said, "*Two British gentlemen, chatty*" and beneath it was a series of dates, all about two years apart. Nothing else.

What are the odds? Doesn't this have to be the gentlemen I just met? If these were the same British guys who visited me just yesterday, then it appears they haven't found what they're looking for yet. And according to this index card, they've been looking for nearly 25 years. Either Jeremy's wife is the most patient person on the planet, or he's lying through his charming accent.

I finally find the espresso-making instructions, sell the customer a Bialetti mocha pot, and resolve to make real espresso myself someday too. (But let's be honest, only if my Keurig pods run out.) In the meantime, I want to get to the bottom of the British gentlemen, but the day's business picks up, and before I know it, I'm wrapping up in a hurry, because tonight's the night.

I'm excited, but if I'm honest, I also have to admit that I believe with all of my heart that Benjamin is going to stand me up. He seems to have appeared in my life from out of nowhere. Guys like him don't just come browsing in a store like mine. I half expect that it's part of a reality show where I'm the dupe.

But just when I'm beginning to despair, Benjamin arrives.

And blame it on my morals. Blame it on desperation. Blame it on those eyes. But the scoop neck sweater and the embroidered jeans are on the floor before our date even officially begins. This is decidedly not the slow-brew approach that Nan would have advised.

Here's what goes down. It all starts when I am innocently showing Benjamin a never-been-opened Kiss record from 1974 that just came in today. He admires the righteousness of their face makeup and then notes that the rhinestones in the album title match the studs in my jeans. Which leads our gaze downward, but before we look at my studded jeans, his eyes stop on my scoop neck sweater.

I have explained that I identify as curvy, but this is a fact that Benjamin may not have noticed when I was wearing a tunic. But he notices now. When he brings his aquamarine gaze back to my eyes, I am all his.

This kiss begins slow and gentle, and he smells of toothpaste and aftershave. His kiss is so delectable that I stand on tiptoe with an aching yearning in me, at which point I lose my balance and he grabs me, but not before a stack of *Better Home and Gardens* cookbooks begins a domino effect with the stack of *National Geographics* next to the *Life Magazines*.

You would think that this avalanche of dusty old

magazines would be the perfect segue to stop making out in my store and go to dinner, but you would be wrong. We restack the magazines and make our way toward the door when we spot the Victorian style chaise tucked away in a secluded corner.

"Have you ever wondered how Victorians did it?" he says.

"You mean with all those crinolines and pinafores and bustles?"

"Yea, and they were always carrying umbrellas, even when it was sunny."

"And wearing silly hats," I say, as he begins kissing me again.

"I'm certain they didn't smell as good as you," he says, nuzzling into my neck.

And what we learn, strictly in the name of historical research and experimentation, is that a Victorian style chaise lounge is in fact the ideal spot for an impromptu romp in an antique store. Maybe those Victorians knew what they were doing after all.

∞∞∞

I'm lying there on the chaise in my post-coital after-glow, imagining a two-car garage and our toddler smiling up at me with Benjamin's blue eyes when he says, "Ah Grace, that was brilliant," with a perfect British accent.

"Now we're British, are we?" I ask.

At which point, he sits up, puts me on his lap—which is no easy feat, mind you—and says, "Actually, I am."

"I don't believe you."

"I could show you my passport," he offers.

"A guy who knows the Fonz, Gilligan's Island, and the Twilight Zone could not be British," I argue.

"What can I say? I love all things kitsch and campy. It comes from my childhood. I spent the better part of my formative years living with my crazy great aunt in the States, when my mum was ill, and all she would do is watch sit-com reruns every night. Got me hooked."

"Okay, well then, a guy who takes a woman to bed before their first date even starts could not be British," I say.

"And why not?" he says, landing a kiss below my neck that sets my nerve endings on fire again.

"It's poor manners. The Brits are all about manners, aren't they?"

"How was my American accent? Did you think I was American?"

"You're changing the subject!"

"I know, but how was it?"

"Not bad. But you could have got me to bed even faster if you had just talked naturally. Don't you know a British accent drives American women wild?"

"You don't think I got you to bed you fast enough?" he says.

"Point taken," I concede.

"I fear our whole relationship is based on a lie," he says, looking honestly contrite.

"Benjamin, we only met three days ago. Can we really say *relationship*? Shouldn't we at least have a date first?"

As I'm locking up the store, he places a kiss on the back of my neck that makes me want to head to the Victorian chaise again. He grabs my hand and shows the way to his car.

If there was any doubt that he was British, his driving settles it. I have to grab the steering wheel and pull us into the right lane three different times on the way to the restaurant. And it's only two miles away.

After a toast with our sake cups in which I, of course, slosh some over the rim and down my hand and wrist, he starts to give me the story. And quite a story it is.

And much as I love gazing into his eyes, I begin to think he is a compulsive liar. A very attractive compulsive liar, whose fingers are wrapping around my knee as he begins to explain.

"You're a sapphire hunter?" I say. "Is that, like, an actual career in England?"

"Not exactly, but it could make or break my career."

Benjamin comes from a family of jewelers in London. Hence his appearance at the jewelry convention in Atlantic City. He says his father, who is too frail to travel, but not too frail to be a controlling son of a bitch, is in search of a sapphire necklace that he designed before Benjamin was born.

"So you weren't shopping for a necklace for your mum then?"

"Nah, my mum's long gone. Lost a long battle with cancer when I was little. I never really knew her, because they shipped me off to live with my great aunt in the States. So I guess that was lie number one," he says. Do compulsive liars admit when they've told a lie? And in that case, are they actually telling the truth? The sake was not helping my head make sense of any of this.

Trying to pull out the truth, I say, "And you're hunting sapphires at my antique shop in the middle of nowheres'ville New Jersey for what reason?"

"I know it sounds far-fetched, but my father had a tip that the sapphire that I'm looking for might be at your store," he explains.

"And that's why you seduced me?" I ask.

"No! The plan was to purchase the sapphire from an old frumpy salesclerk in a dusty old antiques shop who didn't know the importance of the gem and then simply return home. The plan was not to fall head over heels for a gorgeous woman with an encyclopedic knowledge of American pop culture who takes my breath away every time I see her."

What woman would not be bowled over by this? My dilemma becomes clear to me when I realize it is impossible to tell what is a truth and what is a lie.

"What's so special about this particular sapphire necklace?" I ask, trying to maintain some objectivity, but the sake is making me fall deeper into his eyes.

"I don't know. All I know is that if I don't return it to my father, our business could be ruined. He wouldn't tell me anything else."

"And how would a necklace your father designed before you were born end up in my store?" I ask, incredulously.

"He said he had reason to believe it was in your mother's collection, and he read that she had died. He made some calls, learned that her assets were left to her daughter, and figured you might have the necklace but not realize its value."

My mother was just famous enough in her acting roles that her obituary was in the New York Times. But to think that Benjamin's dad was reading my mother's obituary was making my head spin. On the bright side, my mother, may she rest in ever-loving peace, would be thrilled to know that someone in London was reading about her, even if posthumously.

Benjamin's story is still sounding outlandish to me,

but I decide to keep playing along. "And your American accent?"

"Built from years of watching American TV," he says with a proud smile.

"No, not that! I mean *why* did you feel the need to speak with an American accent?"

"Oh that. I wanted to disguise myself in case anyone else came asking. I don't want anyone to know I'm here. Has anyone else come asking about a sapphire necklace?"

"As a matter of fact, they have. Two dapper gentlemen with British accents. They came in the same day you did!"

"That's bad news," he says, looking worried. "We need to find it first."

And suddenly, we are a "we" and I am a sapphire hunter too.

Chapter 10

*"Always keep the key to your heart and the key
to your valuables on separate keychains."*

*N*an loved old keys, especially the old-fashioned bit keys and barrel keys. When I was little, I would look through the basket of keys and wonder where in the world were the doors that these keys once opened. One of the crafters who came by the store regularly used the keys in all sorts of cool projects that she sold on Etsy. Nan and I were so moved when one day she brought us one of her creations. She had added colorful beads, strung together with the keys, to create a windchime that she gave us to hang up outside the store. The tinkling sound the wind chime made on a windy day always made me think of Nan.

Nan always kept the basket of keys near a wooden box full of glass doorknobs. These were popular with people who were restoring old homes. It was one of the many pleasures of owning the store when rehabbers would find just the right matching doorknob for the house they were rehabbing.

But me? I can never keep track of my keys. When I moved into the apartment, the first thing I did was have my locks switched to a keypad. I know Nan wouldn't approve, but give a disorganized girl a hand, you know?

After we finish the last of the pickled ginger slices and Benjamin impresses me with his ability to eat straight wasabi, we head back to my place. His hand starts out on my knee on the ride home, and as sweet as it is, I insist he put it back on the steering wheel. I am relieved when we reach a series of one-way streets where he can't drift into the left lane, and let out a sigh of relief when we pull to a stop.

Benjamin walks me up the steps to my apartment, and before we get to the top step – now keep your minds out of the gutter – you thought I was going to say that we started to do it in the stairwell. We didn't. Before we get to the top step, I notice it. My apartment light is off. I can tell from the crack under the door that it's pitch black.

I always leave my light on. When you live alone, you never know when Freddy Kreuger, Jason Voorhees, or more likely, in my case, that evil doll Anabelle, is going to make an appearance before you have a chance to turn on the lights. Best just to leave them on.

"Maybe the bulb's out?" Benjamin suggests.

We walk out to my car and grab my heaviest snow scraper and the lug wrench from my spare tire compartment.

"Okay, you scrape his eyes out, I'll clock him over the head," Benjamin says.

I can't tell if he's taking me seriously or not, but I give him credit for sticking with me.

He insists on opening the door first, so I punch in the code and he opens it slowly, shouting "Armed police!"

"Armed police? What is this, a British cop show?" I say, laughing. He looks so serious that I can't help feeling this whole thing is surreal.

"Well, what should I shout instead? Stand down, we've got an ice scraper?"

I flip the light switch, and the light comes on, flooding

the apartment in nice, safe rays, and suddenly I'm not so paranoid anymore. We do a quick look around, and everything looks in order. I check all my drawers and cabinets throughout the apartment—which in an apartment this size takes all of 30 seconds—and can't find a thing out of place.

Until I look for Spike. Not in his cage, not under the bed, not in the bathtub where he often likes to curl up, not burrowed under my covers.

There's nothing like an imagined burglary of your apartment and a missing pet rabbit to take the fizzle out of your first date with a hot but possibly delusional chronic liar from England who seemed just minutes ago to want to take you to bed.

Then I start to notice other things slightly out of place. My jewelry drawer, things in my medicine cabinet, my bedside table. Nothing appears to be missing, but nothing seems quite right either. I guess being a small town shop owner of very limited income has its advantages when it comes to getting burgled. In a word, there's nothing worth stealing.

Benjamin walks downstairs with me to check the store. The alarm is still on, and it doesn't appear that anyone attempted to enter the front door or the back door. Maybe it's all in my imagination.

Great, I think, Benjamin is a chronic liar and I am a paranoid freak. But as we head back upstairs, we hear something scratching at the back fire escape door, and a glimmer of hope comes over my face.

"Spike?"

I crack open the door, and a cold bundle of fur hops up the step. I scoop him up and snuggle him.

Nothing is making sense. Is it possible I forgot to turn

on the light before I left? Yes, it's possible. Is it possible that Spike slipped out of my apartment door *and* the building door when I left? Again, possible but not likely. Yet if someone broke into my apartment, why is nothing missing? And wouldn't Spike have hidden rather than bolted? The only person who can answer all of these questions is Spike himself, and he's not even a person. Rabbits are not known as the most reliable witnesses even in the best of circumstances.

Just when I think our first date couldn't get any less romantic than a burglary and a missing rabbit, it does just that. It gets way worse. With Spike nestled safely in my arms, I look up at Ben and he looks positively green.

"I think it was something I ate. I'm allergic to shellfish."

"I don't think you even ate shellfish, did you?"

"No, but you had that avocado and shrimp roll, remember? I think maybe we shouldn't have been making out in the parking lot after that."

"Kissing me made you sick?"

"No, it turned me on! But yes, I think maybe it's also making me sick."

He looks like he's not even going to make it upstairs to my bathroom, but thankfully he does. He ends up staying the night, lying on blankets on my bathroom floor.

I barricade the front door and double-check the windows and sleep with all my clothes on, with the ice scraper on my bedside table. I hear the toilet flushing every hour on the hour.

It is the most upside-down first date I could imagine. Sex, dinner, making out, burglary, vomiting, chastity, in that order.

Suffice it to say, things are not trending in the right

direction.

Chapter 11

"Friends are the cocktails in the bar of life."

I recently acquired a mid-century blue and gold cocktail shaker with six matching tumbler glasses in fairly good condition. You can still see the maker, Culver, Ltd.'s, written in gold script around the top of the shaker, but some of the gold and blue paint is worn off, particularly in the spots where you can picture a person holding it. The set probably belonged to a young couple back in the 1950's or 1960's who would entertain at their house now and then, offering their guests a whole array of cocktails with cool names like Sidecars, Old-Fashioned's, and Manhattans. They'd be saying things like:

"What'll it be, Archie?"

"Make me a sloe gin fizz tonight, baby."

Now, I know that time period was a completely sexist era. Just ask anyone who watched Mad Men, and they'll tell you. So give a girl – excuse me – a woman a break, and don't even get me started on sexism.

But if I could revive one trend of that era – and trust me, only one – it would be the rampant cocktail drinking at any hour of the day for any purpose whatsoever. There's something really kickass about having a platter set up in your living room full of hard liquor just waiting for any random neighbor or delivery person or friend of a friend to stop by and share a cocktail together. Is that too much to ask?

Felicity's jaw drops so far that I can see the chewed up chickpeas and avocado from her quinoa salad. My egg-and-cheese on a toasted bagel is tasting supremely decadent today, but I'm having trouble believing my story myself.

"Right there on that chaise?" she says, with no small degree of admiration.

"I was as surprised as you are!" I say, blushing at the memory. In the light of day, I am somewhat horrified that we christened one of my vendor's sofas. "But you can't tell anyone! My reputation will be tanked!"

"The day you stop worrying about your reputation, Gracie, is the day you achieve freedom, liberation, and true happiness," Felicity says, dabbing the sides of her mouth.

The text I've been waiting for all morning finally chirps in.

Benjamin: Sorry about last night [heart emoji, kiss emoji, vomit emoji]

Who knew that kissing someone who has eaten a shrimp avocado roll with special house sauce can trigger a shellfish allergy? I don't share this part with Felicity. And I don't tell her that my apartment may or may not have been broken into, with the burglar stealing exactly nothing. And I don't tell her that Benjamin is on a quest for a rare sapphire gem. Saying any of these things out loud sounds too absurd.

I decide to give her an annotated, more credible version of our date night and leave it at that. And to tell you the truth, even that doesn't sound so credible.

But I continue anyway, saying, "And there's one more thing that I forgot to tell you. He's British!"

"British! Like with the accent?"

"The whole nine yards – or meters I guess I should say."

"All that and the gorgeous eyes too? I'm so happy for you Gracie!"

And she looks like she truly means it. Between the two of us, let's be honest, she is always the one to get the guy. She's tried to set me up with her boyfriends' friends, but it's usually awkward at best, humiliating at worst. She seems almost as thrilled as I am that I've finally met someone.

She looks at her hands, and then waits a beat to make sure it's okay to move on to a new topic. "I've got some exciting news too. My sister has a wealthy client who loves one-of-a-kind jewelry, and wants me to show her some of my work. She might even commission something from me. I'm going up to meet her on Monday and stay with Suze for a few nights."

I try to look equally happy for Fee, but it fuels my nagging fear. For years she's been talking about her dream of moving to Brooklyn with Suze. Truth be told, I feel jealous of how close she is to her sister. I know that's immature, but losing my grandmother and my mother in the past four years has hit me hard, even if I try not to show it. Fee's the only one who understands.

"That's terrific, Fee! Come out for a drink tonight with me and Benjamin to celebrate."

"No, I can't barge in on your second date!"

"It's not like we haven't broken all the rules of dating already," I say.

"You sure I wouldn't be in the way?" Fee says. She's never been one to turn down the offer of a drink.

"Of course not! Anyway, you've got to meet him and assure me that he's not a serial killer before you go traipsing off to New York without me!"

"You're counting on me to be a judge of character?"

"Wouldn't trust anyone more than you," I say.

∞ ∞ ∞

Benjamin meets me as I'm closing up the shop, and he looks delectable despite the fact that he spent last night heaving up his stomach contents. He leans down to kiss me in the doorway.

"Not so fast, mister! Is there anything else you're allergic to, before I give you another kiss of death?" I say, my finger blocking his lips.

"Just shellfish. Maybe next time we just order a hamburger?" he says, and our lips brush against each other's. Against my better judgement, I'm about to open the door and lead him to the chaise lounge again when I hear Felicity come up behind us.

"Okay lovebirds, don't make me feel like a third wheel. Where are we drinking?"

Our favorite watering hole is a run-down neighborhood bar where the mixed drinks are cheap and the draft beer is even cheaper. The food is terrible, but the best part is that we can walk to it. No designated driver needed. No Ubering home with a strange driver. It's called Duke's Tavern, but everyone calls it Puke's Tavern. I don't share this with Benjamin, considering his fragile state.

George is working the bar tonight. He's known to be heavy handed with the alcohol, especially for young women. Which means I may have to keep an eye on Felicity. She eats like a bird but drinks like a fish, and the combination of the two makes for a very fast buzz.

We are sitting at the bar, with me in the middle, and I am flooded by a feeling of warmth. Benjamin to my left, with his hand on my knee, Fee to my right, brightening up any room she ever enters.

Before long, the conversation moves to jewelry. Benjamin doesn't tell Fee about the lost sapphire, and for a moment, I kind of hope I've dreamed that whole story. He says he's the business manager for his family's jewelry business in London, and he's here in the U.S. on a purchasing trip. I like watching him when he's talking to someone else. He's earnest as a schoolboy when he's talking about business, and he doesn't sound like a chronic liar anymore. He sounds like he knows what he's talking about.

"The jewelry business is all I've ever known. Born with a silver pliers in my mouth, you know? All I remember is my dad hunched over the workbench working into the night. But the honest to god's truth is, I'm crap at the bench. My dad's got some kind of genius for creating pieces that our customers go nuts over, but I don't seem to have inherited any of it. But the business end? I can't say it's all that bad. The clients are rich and demanding, but if you deliver, so do they."

Fee takes out her phone and shows him some of her portfolio. I love her silver work. I pull my hair behind my ears to show him the earrings I'm wearing, crafted of course, by Felicity. They are teardrop shaped with a thin band of silver outlining a jade centerpiece.

Before I realize what's happening, Fee is suddenly in the middle bar stool, drinking her second jack and ginger through the little stirrer straw, and cozying up to Benjamin as he peruses the photos on her phone. I'm on the periphery of their bubble, and to any outsider, it would appear they were a couple. And right now, I'm feeling like that outsider.

"There's only one thing wrong with selling your jewelry in New York," Benjamin says, and Felicity looks up at him with her doe eyes looking pleasantly buzzed. "You need to add a zero at the end of your prices. A New Yorker asking for custom-made jewelry will only be disappointed if it is too affordable."

Benjamin's eyes look warmly at her. She smiles and I can tell she is hooked on him too. It is then that Benjamin – god bless him – circles around to the other empty barstool, putting me in the middle again, and he rests his hand on the small of my back. It feels electric.

When Fee excuses herself to go to the rest room, he turns to me, "I can't do the small talk much longer," he says. "I feel we left things kind of, uh, unfinished last night, don't you?"

And he kisses me right there in Puke's Tavern. I can see George sizing him up. He's been serving me drinks on a regular basis for at least five years, but he's never seen me with a date. I almost think he's going to start clapping for me. Thankfully, he refrains.

I feel Felicity's ring tone go off in my purse, and I look at my phone. I try not to picture her texting me from Puke's unhygienic rest rooms where god knows what transpires.

Felicity: u r right! aquamarine! (sorry for swooning.)
Felicity: now get out of here and get jiggy wit it!

Chapter 12

"If it wasn't important enough for Life Magazine, it wasn't important."

I n Nan's mind, Life magazine was the one and only news source that anyone needed. Never mind that it was photo-journalism, as opposed to actual journalism with things like real words, news, and analysis. Never mind that it only came out once a month. When it stopped publishing altogether, she never exactly found a more modern news magazine to replace it, and I would still catch her every now and then flipping through the old stacks of Life, recalling a different time in her life, a different time in the world.

And she wasn't alone. Every estate sale I've ever attended has a stack of Life magazines that the owner couldn't part with. Some saved only the iconic ones, like with Marilyn Monroe bare-shouldered, or the men walking on the moon, or the young JFK Jr. saluting the hearse. Others kept stacks and stacks of them. We try to keep just a few in the store, mint condition, popular covers, and covers during pivotal years. I have a few of the rarer issues listed on eBay and stored in the back where they are safe from grimy fingers.

When Life was in its heyday, it seemed the media was controlled by just a handful of people who would decide in the editing rooms what got covered and what didn't, who got famous and who didn't, and ultimately who mattered – and *who didn't. Compare that with today's 24-7 access to media and the ability of everyone and her sister to post anything anywhere, and it's no wonder Nan wanted to return to the simpler days where the editors at Life told us all what was important.*

Benjamin nearly trips over Spike when he walks in the door, "Shazbot!" he yells, and Spike cottontails it into my bedroom and hides under the bed.

"Spike, meet Mork from Ork," I say dryly.

"How on earth could you name such a fluffy critter Spike?" Benjamin asks.

"Fun fact," I reply. "Did you know that rabbits' teeth never stop growing? They grow for their entire lives!"

"Interesting," he says, nuzzling his nose into my neck, not unlike Spike does. Fortunately Benjamin does not twitch like a rabbit. "But that still doesn't explain why you'd name him Spike."

"Don't tease him, he's got an unfortunate condition," I say with a gravity that is probably melodramatic, but I like to build up the suspense. I lead Benjamin by the hand to my bedroom, narrating the story as we go.

"Spike was born with an unfortunate malady. He has an underbite, wherein his bottom teeth rest in front of his top teeth. This means that his top teeth never get worn down like other rabbits' teeth do. And because his teeth never stop growing, his top teeth grow – like *Spikes* – right into the bottom of his mouth! I have to take him to the vet once a month to get his teeth filed. Is that the saddest rabbit story you've ever heard?"

But Benjamin isn't paying much attention to Spike's sob story. He's working on my bra clasp and skinny jeans, and I am trying to figure out whether British buttons function the same way ours do. As I'm stepping out of my pant leg, I lose my balance and pull him to the bed with me, trying to make it look intentional, but his leg is tangled in his boxers and we end up butting heads.

"I honestly could fall in love with you Grace, if you could just manage not to kill me first," he says.

We take our time this time around. His kisses are tender and urgent at the same time, and he looks at me so intensely I almost need to look away, but I don't. I learn that I was right about his hands. They are perfect. They know how to tease, how to explore, how to please. My clumsiness gives way to grace as I discover that if I give in to him and trust him, I can move in time with him in a way I never knew possible.

We are delighted to discover that my bed gives us more positional options than the narrow Victorian chaise lounge, and we explore every one of them. Thoroughly. Our slow brew lasts late into the night, leaving poor Spike to quiver himself to sleep.

Together we drift to sleep, the sweetest kind of sleep that makes me feel cozy, secure, and at peace.

Benjamin gives me a kiss first thing in the morning. Correction: it's not morning. It's going on noon and the winter sun is streaming through my curtains. Benjamin has made himself at home in my kitchen. He may not be the master chef of my dreams, but he's heated up a can of baked beans for us and found the toast setting on my toaster oven.

"Do Brits really eat beans and toast for breakfast?" I grumble, with the sleep still in my voice.

"Certainly do, especially if it's already lunchtime!" There are two empty cans on the counter and he sees me eyeing them.

"I gave the rabbit a can of baked beans and he ate them

all!" Spike shuffles over to Benjamin's feet, and he picks him up tentatively.

"Aw, I think he likes you, Benj."

We spend the afternoon plotting out how two novice sapphire hunters who would rather spend more time together in bed are going to find one rare sapphire stone in all of the planet Earth.

"I called my dad yesterday and told him you don't have the necklace. He's quite upset that the sapphire wasn't in your mother's collection. That must mean she sold it or gave it away at some point in her life."

At this moment, the contents of Spike's belly begin to talk back to him. He looks a little rounder than he usually does, although with his winter fur, it's hard to tell, and I can hear a faint gurgling sound.

"Can we back up for a minute?" I say.

"I think Spike might be thinking the same thing," Benjamin quips as a whooshing sound is emitted from beneath the cotton tail.

"I mean can we back up in your story!" I say, rolling my eyes.

"Yes, of course, love," he says. I could get used to the way he calls me love.

"How is it that my mother ever had a piece of jewelry that your dad made? I think we need to start there," I say.

"My dad would only tell me that one of his clients commissioned it. With some of our clients, we need to be rather discreet," he says.

"Ah, like the client was married. But not to her. That kind of discreet?"

"Yes, that would be the kind," he confirms.

"I totally get it. A married guy. That's my mom, to a T. I don't recall her ever hooking up with someone who was actually available. And I know she spent time in London on an acting shoot. But why is this necklace so important? If the client was rich enough to commission a jewelry design in the first place, couldn't he just order a new necklace for his next mistress? And why is your dad the one who wants it back?"

"It's complicated," Benjamin says, and I groan. I can tell there's more to the story that he's not telling me, and I want to believe him, but it's not making sense, and I'm getting frustrated.

"Did you know you're gorgeous when you're angry?" he says, and his hands start roaming underneath my robe – the satin one I've always wanted an occasion to wear. Note to self – burn the terry cloth one with the ketchup stains before Benjamin ever sees it.

It takes all my will power to move his hand away. "Answers, now, Mork from Ork!"

"You're not going to believe me," he warns.

"Try me," I say.

"My pleasure," he says, and begins kissing my neck again.

"Not that kind of trying! I meant tell me what's going on, and I'll see if I believe you!"

Spike ambles over and sniffs Benjamin's toes, which seem to smell just as delectable as the rest of him. I can tell it's tickling his foot, and he picks Spike up and puts him between us.

"What do you think of when you think of England, Grace?" he asks.

"Well, I think of Sherlock, Downton Abbey, Monty Python, the Beatles, David Bowie, you know…"

"Let me rephrase that, what do normal people think about when they think of England? Like Family Feud.

Give me your top three answers."

I love a good game show.

"We surveyed 100 Americans, top three answers on the board...What do you think of when you think of England?"

"Fish and chips?" I guess.

"Survey said? Ding ding ding, number three!"

"Big Ben?"

"Survey said? Ding ding ding, number two!"

"The Royal Family?"

"Survey said? Ding ding ding, number one!"

Benjamin's game has completely distracted me from our conversation at hand. I don't even realize what it means when I have guessed the number one answer.

"The Royal Family, you've guessed it! You know how I said my dad has a gift for designing jewelry? His biggest client is the Crown Jeweler Garrard – the jeweler for the Royal Family!"

"Wait, like Queen Elizabeth, Kate and William, Harry and Meghan?"

"That's the only Royal Family we've got last time I checked," he says.

"You're shitting me," I say.

"See, I knew you wouldn't believe me. But it's true. That's why this is high stakes."

"I still don't get what it has to do with me or my store or my mother," I say.

At that moment, we both startle as the sound of a balloon being pinched at the neck, with a tiny stream of air escaping slowly crescendos between our ears. We look down at Spike and he's shivering and squinting his eyes in a way I didn't know rabbits could do.

"Poor guy seems uncomfortable" Benjamin says, stating the obvious.

"Yes, but thankfully, a rabbit's flatulence is odorless," I say quickly.

But our noses provide a quick rebuttal to that statement. The smell is overwhelming, and I start to wonder how something as small as Spike could produce such a catastrophic odor.

"There's a reason people don't feed their rabbits baked beans!" I say, shoving Benjamin's shoulder away.

"Fortunately baked beans truly are odorless in humans," he says with a hopeful smile as he holds his own rumbling stomach.

He continues with his story. "Like I said, before Spike so unceremoniously interrupted us, my dad was designing a necklace on behalf of one of the nobility – like an earl or a count or baron or something."

"Wait, they still have nobility?"

"Money has a way of reproducing itself, yeah," he says.

"Do they still have Counts? Like Count Dracula?" I say.

"Well, yes, but ours aren't fictional, and they're not from Transylvania," he says.

"Point well taken."

"Anyway, you're distracting me," he says.

"I'm trying," I say, in what I think is my most seductive voice and I flutter my eye lashes a little, but it ends up just looking like I've got something in my eye.

"My dad didn't tell me who the nobility was. He said he believed in confidentiality with his clients," Benjamin continues.

"What, like he's a psychiatrist?"

"More like a priest. He's had his share of confessions by high-ranking adulterers. But anyway, he wouldn't tell me whoever he designed this necklace for, only that the noble guy said he was giving it to your mother. But here's the catch, no pun intended, that he finally explained to me.

"At the same time he was working on your mum's necklace for the philandering noble, the Crown Jewelers sent him the job of a lifetime. The job was to repair one of the most famous pieces of jewelry in the Royal collection. It was none other than Princess Diana's sapphire choker."

"Wait a second," I say, the realization dawning on me. "Are you talking about the sapphire choker with the pearl strands? The one she wore when she danced with John Travolta?"

"That's the one."

"The one she wore with the famous revenge dress?"

"You read too many vintage People magazines."

"Hey, what can I say, I get bored in the store sometimes," I confess.

"But yes you're right, the one she wore with the revenge dress," he says.

"You're still shitting me."

"Apparently the strands of pearls weren't resting exactly right upon her highness's neck and the setting of the sapphire appeared to be grimy after what was termed a 'scuffle' with the paparazzi," Benjamin explains.

"Or perhaps a different kind of 'scuffle' with John Travolta?" I suggest.

"Anything is possible," he says with an eyebrow raised. "Anyway, my father had your mum's sapphire necklace and the Princess's sapphire choker in his shop. He blames it on his assistant, but through some kind of mix-up, the two gems were swapped. Princess Diana's was a 24-carat sapphire of the deepest most pure color, with near-perfect clarity, only two very small inclusions.

While the noble's stone was gorgeous too, it was an artificial sapphire. Lab-created, but to the casual observer, impossible to tell apart from the Princess's stone. The assistant in charge of cleaning the gems must have swapped them. The one in your mother's necklace is the actual stone that the Queen gifted the Princess."

"And the one in the Princess's necklace?"

"The artificial stone intended for your mother."

My head is spinning faster than Benjamin can spin this tale.

"He discovered the mix-up a few years later when he had the choker back in the shop for routine cleaning. He couldn't believe his eyes when he viewed it through the loupe. The inclusions were gone. The lack of any natural inclusions was a dead giveaway that it was synthetic. And by that point, your mother was long gone with the necklace containing the princess's authentic stone, and he had no way of knowing who she was.

"Keeping his mistake a secret ate away at him for years and years. He taught himself how to use the internet specifically so he could search for the sapphire and has been obsessed with finding it. As far as my dad knows, no one else ever knew of the switch. But then he got sick, and that changed everything. He's battling cancer and feels his days are numbered. He wants to make this right before he's too sick to fix it.

"So last year, he talked to the philandering noble who commissioned the necklace for your mum. Made up some ruse and got the noble to tell him the name of the woman he'd gifted the necklace. He had your mother's name and the fact that she was an American actress, and that was all. He began searching for your mother to try to retrieve the necklace. But by then, she herself was ill too and wasn't taking any calls. So that's why he sent me, after he read of your mother's passing."

"And if I had had the necklace?"

"We would have offered to buy it from you for top dollar, whatever you wanted."

"And you promise that getting into my panties wasn't in the plan?"

"It wasn't in the initial plan, but I'm nothing if not adaptable," he says with that half-smile.

"If no one else knows about the switch, then who were those two dapper guys searching for sapphires in my store last week?"

"I dunno. And I didn't have the heart to tell my dad about them. He's already worried enough that he won't be able to find the stone."

"I still think you're shitting me."

"I would never shit you," he says. Now, I ask you, could a man petting my gaseous rabbit Spike so tenderly on his lap really be lying to me?

"Can we take a break and go back to the part where you try me?" I suggest.

Benjamin is all too happy to oblige.

Chapter 13

"Never put your secrets in writing."

I remember sorting through the mix of junk, vintage items, and collectibles that Nan had purchased at an auction from an estate. Most of what the deceased old woman owned was beyond salvage, but Nan had wanted a particular table lamp that was grouped in with a whole lot of miscellaneous items. She put me to the task of separating the wheat from the chaff. This was back when I was still living in New York, still fancying myself a writer. One of the items the woman had left behind was her diaries. I debated for several days—okay, let's be honest, several seconds—as to whether it was ethical to read them. I knew it wasn't, but all the same I cracked open one of them, and then another, and another. I told myself they could be fodder for my next short story, as long as I kept the old woman's name out of it.

I searched and combed those diaries for a scrap of a storyline. But I ended up with nothing. Turns out the life of a retired woman in a small New Jersey town isn't all that interesting. And in the end, I felt I had violated her trust. In fact, uncovering the mundane monotony of her life was almost more of a violation than finding something salacious.

That was the point when I shredded all of my own writings and journals. You can't write creatively without writing yourself into it, without revealing a hidden side of yourself, *and those are secrets I just don't want to share.*

Like all good things, our tryst comes to an end almost as quickly as it began. I drive Benjamin to the airport the next morning and make out with him in the car like we're teenagers until—no joke—a security agent knocks on the passenger side window. I drop Benjamin at the terminal and watch his back retreating through the revolving doors. He's got appointments with rare gem dealers and auction houses throughout the southwest and west coast with stops in Santa Fe, Los Angeles, San Francisco, and Las Vegas.

I tell him I will put the word out to other antique dealers and auctioneers I know, in search of a 24-carat sapphire. But he looks at me with the resigned expression of someone looking for a needle in a haystack, a grain of sand in a desert, a drop of water in the ocean, well, you get the idea.

Will I see Benjamin again? I feel so all-consumed with him now, that it's hard to believe he will just vanish. But as his figure turns a corner and steps out of my view, and as I sit all alone in my second-hand Dodge Charger, it immediately feels like a dream that never happened.

With Fee out of town and the store closed today, I settle back into my apartment to assess what to do next. Whenever I need to think and to really focus, my best bet is to rearrange. Rearranging my living room is one of my favorite pastimes.

For all my love of antiques, kitschy 70s tchotchkes, and television memorabilia, my apartment is modern, sleek, and uncluttered. I get my fill of clutter working the antique shop, and coming upstairs to a clean and crisp apartment gives me a sense of calm and order.

The sleek design of all the best luxury brands is how I

envision my living space, but in the reality of my bank account, we are talking Ikea. And if I am not entirely thrilled with all that Ikea has to offer, I can say this. It is versatile. And pleasant to hang out with. Over the years, I feel like I've befriended a whole host of Scandinavian friends, like Vittsjö my sofa, Kivik my end table, Trulstorp my light fixture, my Brimnes bed, and of course my BFF, Bestå my television stand. I tell all these friends it's time for a change, and with a little pushing, shoving, and sliding, I have a newly styled living room by mid-afternoon. But still no answer to my dilemma of what to do next.

And here's my dilemma.

I have the sapphire necklace.

Yes, you heard me right. I have the sapphire. And if my very cute instantaneous British boyfriend with the aquamarine eyes is telling the truth, it belongs to the late Princess Diana.

Hence the dilemma.

This is a dilemma that I did not know I had until lover boy walked into my life last week. Call me unromantic, but just because my vintage-loving 70's sitcom-quoting soulmate has found me on this large planet and made me feel whole for the first time in my life doesn't mean I have to tell him everything, does it?

And let's not be naïve, I tell myself. When I met Benjamin, he was acting. Like he told me, our relationship started out with a lie. If I can't trust his accent, then what can I trust? I start to wonder whether he really does love *Welcome Back Kotter* and know all the words to My Sharona. Were these lies too?

I sink into Vittsjö's cushions and curl up with Spike and a cup of tea. I'm not normally a tea drinker. Honestly, it tastes like what might come out of the bottom of my composter, if I were eco enough to keep a composter. When it comes down to it, what is tea after all? Dead leaves. Just like compost. And who would think drinking hot compost water is a good idea?

But in the spirit of keeping my British shag in my memories, the tea seems to be the right choice. In the movies, Brits always heat up the tea kettle when there's any hint of a dilemma, and I want to explore whether this sorry substitute for coffee helps me to get to the bottom of my dilemma.

I start by asking myself, which is more preposterous? My mother accidentally getting Princess Diana's sapphire? Or me getting the cute guy?

And it is then that it dawns on me that of all the unbelievable things Benjamin has been telling me, the most unbelievable to me is that he would find me attractive. Let's face it, in real life, the curvy women do not get the cute guys. It just doesn't happen.

And if his attraction to me was all an act, that means the Princess Diana story must be his real motive. Ergo, it might actually be true. And if it is true, then he is acting out in real life the plot of one of the greatest Indiana Jones rip-off movies ever: *Romancing the Stone*. And that makes me Kathleen Turner circa 1994. I could do worse.

Which brings me to the question: Is Benjamin trying to steal the necklace from me? What about the two British gentleman? How do they know about the necklace too? Is there anyone I can trust?

"I haven't always known about the necklace," I begin to tell Spike, by way of confession. "In fact," I say, "I still have trouble believing it is real."

Spike is only half listening. It seems to be his bath time again.

So I retreat into my own head, replaying the story that led me to this point...

When my mother died, I was overwhelmed with the sole responsibility of being her executor. I had to box up her belongings, get her townhouse cleaned and ready for sale, and run the antique shop all the while. It wasn't until about two months ago that I made it to the bank to claim the items in her safe deposit box.

I still remember my annoyance at the older bespectacled teller who seemed downright inconvenienced to have to read over my legal documents and let me into the secured area. He smelled like moth balls, and it didn't look like it would be long before I might be browsing his belongings in one of the estate sales I so often frequented for *Antique Junction & Etc.* He hovered over my every move and kept a sour expression on his face the entire time.

When I finally made it through the red tape and the ornery bank teller, the safe deposit box contained ten savings bonds that had matured, giving me an unexpected windfall, which after taxes, helped me pay off a few more of my mom's bills. Also in the box were our birth certificates, social security cards, an old mortgage document from the tiny row house we had lived in, and a term life insurance policy that had expired ten years earlier.

I stared at my birth certificate. It's something I always knew, but seeing the "unknown" scrawled in a simple black ballpoint pen where a father's name might be hit me hard this time. I never once wished my father were in my life. My Nan and my mom were all I needed. As far as I was concerned, we had a perfect trifecta. But with both of them gone, I felt the enormity of carrying on without them.

What broke me out of my funk was finding an ordinary-looking yellow cardboard necklace box from a once-famous Philadelphia department store called Strawbridge and Clothier. It showed a few signs of age but otherwise looked utterly unremarkable. But when I opened it, an extraordinarily luminescent gem nearly blinded me. I made an audible gasp. The first thing anyone would notice about the stone was that it was enormous. It was cut round but styled in an almond-shaped platinum setting. The setting rested in the middle of a bar of diamonds. On each side of the sapphire were six diamonds, getting gradually smaller as they blended into the platinum necklace links. Simply put, it was tremendous.

So naturally, the first thing I did was show it to Felicity. I needed to know if it was the real deal.

"Incredible," she whistled, looking through her jeweler's loupe. "It looks like the friggin' Hope Diamond!"

"Aw, don't say that, Fee. The last thing I need is a cursed necklace," I pleaded.

"Definitely pure sapphire," she said. "I can see two small inclusions."

"English, please."

"Inclusions are the little imperfections that occur as sapphire is being formed underground. Real sapphires, meaning the ones that are mined, almost always have inclusions. Fake sapphires are made in labs, and don't have these markings."

"Everyone needs a jeweler friend like you, Fee."

"Enough gem education, Grace. The point is, I. CAN. NOT. IMAGINE. how much this necklace is worth!"

Not knowing what to do with this unexpected treasure, we agreed that it would be safest to keep it in a safe, which I did not own, given that I traded mainly in costume jewelry. Felicity showed me which kind to order, and we stowed the necklace in her jeweler's safe for the time being.

"Having this thing is making me nervous, Grace. I don't think I've ever had something so valuable in my house!" she said, the day my own safe arrived. So to celebrate the awesomeness of the necklace, and to learn how to use my new digital mini-safe, which required programming in my fingerprint and entering Fort Knox-level passcodes, Felicity invited me over for a holiday fest. We had decided to hold our own holiday party for two, where we would get dressed in our finest, and drink more holiday cocktails than was good for us.

We found vintage party dresses at my shop. Mine was way too tight and showed cleavage that might only barely be legal, but it was the perfect neckline for the necklace. I looked stunning, if I do say so myself. We ordered takeout, mixed fruity vodka drinks, and binge-watched romantic comedies until I was convinced Matthew McConaughey was my destiny.

Next we began fantasizing about where my mother might have gotten the gorgeous necklace that graced my collar bones. I let Fee try it on too, and of course she rocked it.

"Romance with a rich movie star, from her acting days?" Felicity guessed.

I shrugged my shoulders. My mother's boyfriends never seemed to be particularly wealthy, and it seemed they never stuck around long enough to want to buy her fine jewelry.

"Maybe she just splurged on it at Tiffany's. She was a jewelry fiend."

"Where would she have gotten that kind of money to

buy it?" Fee asked.

"The lottery? Court settlement? Inheritance from her father, the asshole whose name Nan never let me so much as whisper?"

"I can't believe she never wore it, and never showed it to you. She never even told you she had it?" Felicity asked.

"Nope. Not a word," I said. "But come to think of it, where on earth *could* you wear this thing? It's not exactly everyday jewelry that you could wear to the grocery store, you know?"

"And it's not like her boyfriends ever took her anywhere nice on a date, according to you. Didn't you say the one guy took her to KFC on their first date?" Fee remembered.

We drained the remainder of the vodka bottle, and somehow in the drunkenness of the moment, we managed to sort out the instructions for the mini-safe and Fee walked me back in the dead of the night to my apartment, where I stowed the safe, cleverly, I thought, in the middle of a stack of toilet paper.

But last week, when the two British gentleman and Benjamin came into the shop on the same day asking about purchasing sapphire necklaces, my paranoia rose up like a cloud of vape smoke, and I realized I had used most of the stack of toilet paper, leaving my mini-safe in clear view to anyone who opened my cabinet door.

"Fee, what good is a mini-safe if someone could just steal the whole thing?" I asked over the phone. She agreed.

So I asked Jakob—the Sisterhood's private handyman and jack of all trades— to help me fasten the safe to the bottom of my bathroom cabinet, behind the tower of feminine products and beside my Ekloøn trash can that fit so neatly in the vanity.

Just in the nick of time too, I thought. When I thought someone had broken into my apartment on the night of my first date with Benjamin, the bathroom was the first place I checked. The safe was undisturbed, as was everything else in my apartment, except for Spike going missing.

I still am not sure if anything happened that night, but I feel more secure knowing that the safe is bolted in place.

"So that's the story, Spike," I say to a sleeping pile of fur next to me. He exhales a big sniff and appears to agree with me that it's a bit of a mystery.

"Do I tell Benjamin I have the sapphire, or do I keep up the charade that I'm helping him find it?"

Spike doesn't say a word.

Chapter 14

"There's a thin line between beauty and disgrace."

One item in our store that doesn't necessarily sell well, but still fascinates me to this day is our hand-carved duck decoys. Nan liked them too and believed they were a deeply unappreciated art form. To give them their due, we would play a little game with them. We would hide our favorite decoy – a mallard drake carved with the finest of details so as to look realer than a live duck – in different spots throughout the store, kind of like a precursor to the more popular elf on the shelf game. We wouldn't tell each other when we found it or when we hid it. It would just keep showing up in different places. If I had hid it most recently, I would try my best to walk nonchalantly past the hiding space, although more often than not, I would start to smile just enough that Nan knew where to look. Once Nan removed it from my hiding spot, it would take me weeks to find it again. She was crafty at hiding things.

I always thought so fondly of these intricately carved ducks. Once we even had a decoy swan in the shop. The customer who bought it was so delighted to find it that she named it after Nan and displayed it prominently in her beach bungalow.

Truly these carved ducks were works of art, and they held a special place in my heart until one day I learned their real purpose. I knew that they were called decoys, and that made *sense to me. They weren't real ducks after all. But it was only after overhearing Jakob talking to a customer one afternoon that I learned their purpose was to lure real ducks into a sense of safety so that hunters could shoot them! How could something so beautiful be used for so nefarious a purpose? It's a disgrace. To this day, I never sell them to hunters. I ask any customer to assure me they are using the beautiful ducks for decorative purposes only. It's only right. Right?*

It's early in the morning, and no one is in the store yet. I'm just about to flip the closed sign to open when Geena arrives with a beaded shoulder bag and a cup of coffee the size of a small pitcher.

"G'morning Gracie!" she says with a warm wide smile that spans the many years that she has known me. Nan always said that she and Geena were the original founders of the Sisterhood. The Sisterhood, as I came to know it over time, was anyone who passed Nan's inspection as a woman you could trust. And this included Jakob, his gender excused due to his unequivocal strength of character. I once asked Nan if I was finally old enough to become a member of the Sisterhood, but she told me every woman needs to develop her own sisterhood using her own set of values and criterion. That's something I was still working on, but I was pretty sure Fee was my co-founder.

"Got some receipts for you, Geena," I say. "A retro mom was in the store yesterday. You would've loved her. Bought up your whole collection of ViewMasters and your Weebles set for her twins."

"It's only a matter of time 'til her kids discover Atari, and then it's all over," Geena says.

I laugh at the thought of today's kids playing on a lo-tech Atari console. It would feel ancient to them.

"I think it was too late already," I say. "Both kids were

fighting over their mom's smartphone. They're already beyond Atari, let alone the lowly ViewMaster their mom was trying to foist on them."

Geena takes her receipts and adds a couple more items to her display. A monopoly game from the 1960's in pristine condition and a crocheted sweater with patches as large as potholders.

Next I show her the newest estimate from the contractor, who is going to start work soon on the store renovation. I was so excited about it last week, but I think Geena can tell my heart isn't in it right now.

"What's on your mind pumpkin? I can see you're preoccupied with something," she says. She's always been able to read me like a book. "Boy troubles?"

"Not troubles, not really. But I did meet someone," I say. "That's not something that happens to me every day."

"The cute guy who was pacing outside the store the other day?"

"Yep, that's the one. Benjamin."

Geena pulls up a metal folding chair and opens it up behind the counter. When she takes the lid off her coffee, I can smell the hazelnut flavoring and it reminds me of how she and Nan used to bicker over the merits of plain black coffee versus sweetened flavored coffee.

"It's probably just puppy love, but he really seemed like someone I could click with," I say.

"*Seemed*? You mean it's over already?"

"Not over, but he lives in England! So, yes, I guess it's over before it even really began."

"People have long-distance relationships, Grace. In fact, how do you think Reggie and I lasted as long as we did? He is barely ever home, that's how! How'd you leave things with this guy?"

"He's still in the U.S. for business. He's on the west coast now, and I'm hoping he stops to see me again before his flight home. He's been texting me like I'm the love of his life. Keeps saying how gorgeous I am. But I don't know, Geena. There's something I just don't trust about him."

"What don't you trust? You afraid you're gonna get hurt?"

"Yes, I guess that's part of it. But you saw him, Geena. He's to die for. Bedroom eyes, tussled hair, athletic build. Guys like that don't go for me. I guess I don't trust that someone like him would really want to be with me."

"That's not something you don't trust about him, pumpkin; that's something you don't trust about yourself. When someone tells you that you're gorgeous, you gotta learn to drink that in. In all the years I've had the pleasure of knowing you, you have been nothing but gorgeous. I'm not surprised at all that Benjamin sees it. Now if only you can see it too," Geena says.

"But there's more. I've been lying to him about something," I say.

"Now who's the untrustworthy one?" Geena asks.

"Yea, that would be me, and I'm worried that he won't forgive me, so I don't know how to tell him," I say.

"Never too late to start telling the truth," Geena says.

Geena's never steered me wrong before, so I take her advice. I can't expect things to go anywhere with Benjamin if I am hiding the truth from him. I'll just have to take the leap of faith that he's being truthful with me, crazy as his story sounds. I text him while he's in flight.

Me: Facetime me when you check into your hotel room. Got something important to tell you.

Benjamin: Oh no! Sounds ominous...like, you're actually married with children?

Me: No!

Benjamin: You've met someone else?

Me: No, you've only been gone four hours!

Benjamin: A lot can happen in an antique store in less than four hours. Trust me, I know.

Me: True enough!

Benjamin: <kiss emoji>

Me: I should run an ad campaign on the benefits of Victorian chaises

Benjamin: You could make millions. Do it!

Me: <heart emoji> <fire emoji>

A group of three women enter the store, one pushing her sunglasses up onto her head, her hair flowing in perfect waves, and stowing her car keys in her handbag. I like to watch women shopping together to observe their patterns. Groups of three are especially interesting, because our aisles are a little tight for three people to browse together comfortably. Will they stay together anyway? Or will they split up into a faction of one versus two? Will they talk much?

This group starts out together, but eventually migrates out so that each woman is shopping alone. They seem caught up in their own reminiscences as I see them pick up items, turn them over, and put them back down. It's hard to tell whether their expressions are tired or bored, or whether they simply wear the faces of women of a certain age, but I see no smiles, just a seriousness that I hope I don't fall into at their ages.

This all changes when the woman with the sunglasses discovers a find, calling the other two friends over. Their faces come alive and their eyes light up.

"Look, this looks just like the pottery you had in your house growing up!" she says to her blonde friend with the high ponytail.

"It is! Hadley pottery. Remember we had the horse collection?"

The dark-haired woman pipes up. "Yes! I loved the horse plates. I remember eating off those plates at your dining room table, whenever your Dad cooked up something delicious for us."

"I love how they're so whimsical. The sailboat – it's so simple, yet it just makes me smile."

Their conversation continues and I realize that I am eavesdropping on another sisterhood. These women seem to have known each other all their lives. I find myself wondering what they were like as little girls growing up together. Having a Dad who cooked meals, playdates where they got invited over for dinner, the different twists and turns of their lives that brought them here to my store on this chilly January day.

"But you don't even know the story behind the plates," the blonde woman continues, now talking animatedly with her hands. "My dad, when he lived in Kentucky, was studying art, and apprenticed under Mary Alice Hadley at her pottery company. Those plates were really special to him."

I chime in with a little trivia I know about the pottery, hoping they don't mind that I've been hearing their conversation. "Some of the most gorgeous pottery comes out of Kentucky. Apparently that area had some of the best ancient clay deposits, and Louisville became a center for pottery making back in the old days,"

I immediately regret saying "ancient" and "old days," not wanting to insult my customers. They don't seem to notice.

They ask me to open the case so they can look at the pottery more closely. I have only three mismatching M.A. Hadley items. The sailboat bowl, the lighthouse plate, and the whale mug. The friends each agree to buy one to keep the memory of the blonde woman's father in their homes.

As the doorbells tinkle on their way out the door, I think to myself about their sisterhood. The comfort and trust they have with each other is almost palpable.

As I'm closing up the shop, I'm beginning to think Geena is right. It's time for me to start trusting. Trusting myself. Trusting my friends. Trusting Benjamin.

Now that I've decided, I can't wait until Benjamin calls. He will be so happy to see the necklace. After work, I raid my closet and find a silky off-white v-neck, which is nondescript enough to give the sapphire necklace center stage. Spike follows me around as I pad about.

I plan to start out our Facetime with the camera focused on Spike, and doing a silly Spike voice to get Benjamin warmed up. Then I will rotate the camera around to focus on me, and just wait for Benjamin to notice that I am wearing the necklace. He will be so thrilled. I know he will forgive me for not telling him immediately.

Next I rummage under my bathroom cabinet and pull out my packages of overnight sanitary napkins and tampons. And behind them, resting safely, bolted to the bottom of the cabinet, is my trusty mini-safe where I have been storing the necklace.

The night I thought I was burgled, I had to check on the mini-safe without Benjamin noticing me, but all it took was a quick reach into the cabinet to feel the cool steel of the safe with its door still shut. Now I am congratulating myself for camouflaging it behind my sanitary products as I place my fingertip over the touchID to unlock it.

But as the door to the safe pops open, I suddenly feel a wave of nausea come over me, and my hand feels like it is in a movie, moving in stylized slow-motion into the cavern of the safe. I somehow know it before my hand can even confirm it. My stomach drops and my mind starts to spin. I can't believe it, and I can believe it, all at the same time. The necklace is gone. The safe is completely empty. I run my hand around the interior. I squat down and stare into the safe. I toss out everything, the towels, tampons, toilet paper, the Q-tips, everything until the cabinet is empty. No necklace. For good measure, and in true Grace style, I crash my head into the top of the bathroom cabinet as I am standing up.

The first thing I think is: Holy hell my head hurts!

The second: I really was burgled.

The third: This safe is a cheap piece of shit. How the hell could someone have opened it?

Within ten minutes, I hear the Facetime call. It's Benjamin of course, and I have no necklace to show him. Would he believe that I had the necklace, but that it got stolen out of my locked safe? Now I'm the one with a crazy-ass story. And I'm not ready to share it with him.

"Hey love," he says, looking tired but still ruggedly handsome after the ten-hour plane journey with two layovers. He gives me a brief Facetime tour of his hotel room, and I begin to fantasize about being there with him. He shows me palm trees out the window and tells me how warm it was when he stepped out of the airport. I wrap my sweater tighter around me.

"What is it you needed to tell me?" he asks, sounding a little nervous.

This is the point where I was going to show him the necklace. Since I have no Plan B, I just go with my heart.

"Just that I'm crazy over you," I say.

I have learned the hard way not to say these types of things out loud. In my past relationships, the minute I ventured into telling someone how I felt, the guy had one foot out the door. But this time, I'm going on trust. Trusting in myself. Trusting in him.

"Phew, Grace. I thought you were splitting up with me! You coulda texted me and saved me the suspense. The whole rest of the plane ride I was a mess."

"Didn't I heart and fire emoji you?"

"Yes, at first those emojis were enough, but then I started to think the emojis meant that you wanted to burn my heart to the ground, and I kind of spiraled downhill after that. How do I know that emojis mean the same thing to Americans as they do to Brits?"

"I didn't know. I'm sorry Benj!"

"No, no, don't be sorry. You know what, Grace?"

"What?"

"I'm crazy over you too."

After the call, I sit down on Vittsjö and stare into space, stunned. Spike joins me, and given the predicament I am in, I realize that Spike is the only person I can talk to about this. And he's not even a person.

All of this creates a new wrinkle in my rapidly unfolding dilemma, a dilemma fast becoming a mystery. On one hand, I don't feel as guilty for not telling Benjamin that I had the necklace, because now that lie has become a truth. But on the other hand, who does have the necklace? And whose sapphire is it in the first place? Mine, or the late Princess Diana's?

As far as I know, there are only four people who are

desperate for the sapphire: Benjamin, Benjamin's father, and the two British men who visited the store. Who could have stolen it? Benjamin was with me all evening, so that narrows it down to three. Benjamin's father is deathly ill in England, or so Benjamin tells me. So that narrows it down to the two old British gentlemen, who, according to Nan's index card, have visited the store every two years for the past decade. But even with this short list of suspects, I can't bring myself to call the police. I barely even believe the story myself. But whether or not Benjamin's story is true, how could the necklace be removed from the safe without my fingerprint? It has to be the two gentlemen, but how?

All I know is that now one thing is clear. I want to get to the bottom of this mystery and get the necklace back. And therefore, with my right hand raised and my left hand on the latest copy of Elle magazine, I take a solemn pledge and inaugurate myself as a newly-instated member of the Order of Sapphire Hunters. And this time, Benjamin, I believe.

Chapter 15

*"Stay two steps ahead. That's all
it takes. Just two steps."*

*N*an loved board games. I guess there wasn't much else to do in her childhood growing up before screens took over our lives. But me? I barely had the patience for board games. She liked to try to build my concentration by playing Master Mind with me. It's a decoding game, with a little touch of strategy and scheming thrown in.

When it was my turn to be the master, and I was waiting for her to make her next guess at my secret code, I would often sit transfixed by the photograph on the cover of the game. It depicted a debonair white man wearing a gray suit with cufflinks at his wrists. Only a girl like me who grows up in an antique shop knows what cufflinks are anymore, but to me, they symbolized wealth, sophistication, intelligence, refinement, and well, a certain level of asshole. His fingers were tented together and his head was tilted at an angle that suggested wisdom or at least narcissism. The top of his hair was an unusual shade of orange, not garish like Trumpian hair, yet strange nonetheless, while the sides had grayed.

What caught my eye most was the woman standing behind him. She appeared to be of southeast Asian descent, wearing an ill-fitting cream colored sleeveless dress, long hair, bangs, and staring seriously into the camera. The look on her face said that she could kick your ass if she weren't wearing this stupid cocktail dress. Her left arm was on the back of his armchair, and she was leaning toward the man, creating a triangular shape.

The two were posed above a glass table that was so shiny and clean that it beamed back their reflection, but I always felt the photographer should have placed them closer to the table, because as it stood, the man's reflection was cut off right under his bottom lip, and the woman's head was cut off completely in the reflection.

What did all this mean? Were they a couple? Were they competitors? Which one of them was the mastermind? Was this casting an early attempt at diversity in advertising? Or was there a racist slight that I didn't quite understand here? It baffled me more than the game itself.

But I digress. My point being, Nan tried to teach me how to stay two steps ahead via the Master Mind game—the self-professed game of cunning and logic. Did it work? It remains to be seen. But I'm gonna try.

Now that I am a certified sapphire hunter, I need to get down to business. First thing in the morning, I head down to the store, and begin searching determinedly through my receipts, my junk mail, and my notes to my-self. I know I saved it somewhere, and at last, hiding between the cash register and a tape dispenser, I find what I'm looking for: the folded yellow post-it note where Jeremy had jotted down his number.

It goes to voicemail, as I expected, but it's no help. His greeting simply identifies him as Jeremy and is followed by a pleasant "cheerio!" I was hoping to learn his last name. I hang up on the voicemail greeting and start composing in my head the message I want to leave. I rehearse the message, but before I can dial again, my cell starts ringing. It's him. I'd better think fast if I want to get his last name.

"Hi Jeremy, it's Grace, from *Antique Junction & Etc.* Any luck on finding the right sapphire necklace for your wife?" I ask, playing it dumb.

"Why? Have you found something I might like?" he asks, sounding decidedly nervous.

"Not exactly, but I've been talking with a dealer in, uh, Miami, who my mom used to work with. His name is John. She was a bit of a jewelry afficionado before she passed away last year. He said he's still got some of her jewelry in his store, including a sapphire necklace, and he'd be happy to give you a call. He can send you photos and the stats on it. Would you like to talk with him?"

"Why certainly, so kind of you to ask, that would be brilliant," he says, sounding markedly more excited than when our conversation began.

"Serious customers only, he told me. And fair warning – this one is authentic and won't be cheap. Could I get your first and last name for him?"

"It's Jeremy Robinson, and yes, yes, that would be lovely."

"Terrific," I say. "And, oh, apologies, a customer is coming in the door now. I gotta run, but I'll text you the dealer's number in case you don't hear from him. And as you would say, cheerio!"

Mission accomplished: I've got his first and last name. And of course there is no customer coming through the door. The lies are coming easier and easier for me.

Next up I search through last week's receipts and find it within minutes. It turns out that Jeremy's friend who bought the cookbooks was Ian Walker, according to his credit card. Bingo, I've got his first and last name too.

I jot down the names Jeremy Robinson and Ian Walker on Nan's old index card and I'm pretty pumped. If Benjamin and I can track down these two men, we may be a step closer to finding the sapphire. All I have to do is get Benjamin to agree to be the fictitious Miami jewelry dealer, and Jeremy and Ian should come to us.

But my elation fades quickly when I realize how common these names are. There must be millions of people with these names. It makes me wonder if these really are their true names.

Undaunted, I give Benjamin a call.

"Hi love," he says with a groan. "I want to thank you for calling at five in the morning. There's nothing that makes me happier than five o'clock in the morning."

Shit, I forgot he's three hours behind.

"You seemed pretty happy at my place at five o'clock in the morning," I remind him.

"When it's five o'clock in the morning and you've been up since the previous evening with a beautiful woman sitting naked on top of you, yes that's different," he agrees. "Can we try that again sometime, then?"

I take this as an encouraging sign that there is *not* a California girl sitting naked on top of him at this particular five o'clock in the morning. I tell him about Jeremy and Ian.

"Excellent work, Gracie! I told you you'd make a good sapphire hunter," he says.

"But their names are as common as the common cold," I say, suddenly feeling that it wasn't worth calling him.

"That's where algebra comes in, my dear," Benjamin says.

"Algebra?" I say. "Everyone knows that algebra has no

purpose in the real world."

"Sure it does!" he says. "We've now got two of our variables figured out. We just need to find out what equation we're talking about."

"Come again?" I say.

"Would love to."

"Mind out of the gutter, please!"

"Sorry, love. What I mean is that finding any one of these fellows with a very common name would be difficult. But having both of their names together will narrow our search."

"Oh, so like if I google Jeremy Robinson I'll get 5 trillion results, whereas if I google Jeremy Robinson and Ian Walker together, I'll only get 3 trillion results."

"Something like that."

"One other wrinkle," I say. "Would you care to impersonate a jewelry dealer in Miami for me?"

He's thrilled at the chance to use his American accent again and agrees to set up a voicemail as John, the Miami jewelry dealer who has my mom's sapphire necklace, and while at it, uncover whatever it is that Jeremy and Ian know about the necklace. At this point, I feel like we're a pretty good team of sleuths.

"I like sapphire hunting with you," he says sleepily before hanging up.

I hang up too, feeling that maybe I am the original Master Mind. My strategy is this: if Jeremy does not call John the fictitious jewelry dealer, that means Jeremy stole the necklace and has no need to search for it anymore. And if he does call the fictitious dealer, then we are one step closer to figuring out why someone else is looking for the necklace, which could possibly get us closer to finding out who does actually have it.

Either way, we learn something, and for the time being, I don't have to reveal to Benjamin that I once had the necklace. I don't know why I'm holding onto this. It's that one part of me that still doesn't fully trust Benjamin. Am I wrong?

Chapter 16

"Nothing's finer than a diner."

One of the collections I've always loved at Antique Junction & Etc. is the old postcards. Somewhere along the line, Nan ended up becoming the one-stop source for postcards of long-gone New Jersey diners. I loved flipping through the postcards during quiet times at the store. The diners always featured a photo of the enormous garish signs that were as tall as the local ordinances allowed. Fresh pastries baked daily on the premises! Air conditioned! Fresh brewed coffee!

My favorite diners of course were the stainless steel ones that looked like they were fashioned out of an Airstream trailer, like the Neptune Diner. Whoever's idea it was to make a diner out of stainless steel deserves an award. Our Neptune Diner postcard showed the diner with this awesome neon sign, including a neon version of the god Neptune who appeared to be ruling over the ocean wielding his trident in one hand while grilling up your dinner with the other.

I also loved the postcards that showed cars parked outside the diners. The cars from the 1950's were boxy, ballsy, and made of some seriously heavy metal. Some would have the tail fins, jutting out like wings getting ready for flight. Others would have that decorative feature in the back that looked to me like a jet engine. But most were just run-down jalopies. I could get lost in thought looking at these old *photos, just imagining the customers stepping out of those grand cars, admiring the shine of the chrome around their round taillights as they came around the back of the car, letting out their date from the passenger seat. Once inside, putting a coin in the jukebox, ordering a plate of scrambled eggs for all of eighty-five cents, along with a plain black coffee, before anyone in New Jersey knew what a latte was.*

The postcards weren't huge sellers, but customers enjoyed perusing them, and I was always a little sad to see one leave the collection when someone purchased it.

With Fee still in New York, the night is a toss-up between drinking by myself at Duke's Tavern and hanging out with Spike. The choice is obvious. Spike isn't much of a conversationalist, so I decide to tackle the project I've been avoiding. Going through my mother's remaining boxes. The remaining odds and ends are the kind of thing that I can't quite part with. But they're too personal to donate, and I don't know what I'd actually do with them if I kept them. Her high school yearbook, a few scarves I remember her wearing but would never wear myself, an aging baby doll that she'd saved but is even too deteriorated to sell in the store, her favorite coffee mug that I feel strange drinking from now that she has passed. It's just hard to know what to do with these things.

I brew a cup of Earl Grey Tea, in honor of Benjamin, who is beginning to feel like a surreal dream, and curl up on Vittsjö with Spike and one of my mother's photo albums. My plan is to take pictures of her old photos and upload them into her collection of digital photos, once I find her password, and then import them all into my own photo stream.

The earliest photos show my mother in her twenties, at the height of her acting career, and me as an infant.

I remember looking through this album as a little girl. I always assumed I would grow up to look like her, the Audrey Hepburn jaw line, the almond shaped eyes, the petite figure. I loved to sit with her and listen to her stories of the TV business. The auditions, the scripts, the smarmy directors, the endless takes, the thrill of seeing the final edit.

Looking at the photo album today, I feel something different that hadn't registered on me before. I see a rich and full life of friends, boyfriends, travels, and dining. Her eyes are bright and hopeful. Her magnetism jumps off the page. And as I progress in the album, the photos of her infant girl start to fill the pages. (That's me, in case you hadn't worked that out.) What few photos there are of my mother, her eyes have lost the shine. To be fair, raising me as a single mom had to be exhausting. But more than simple fatigue, it seems a light has gone out in her eyes.

The one photo where the light in her eyes has returned is one that Nan snapped at the international airport, when my mom took a solo trip around England and Europe. She was away for two weeks. I was in high school at the time, and I looked at it as an extended vacation away from my mom, with only Nan to answer too. The look in Mom's eyes in this photo makes it look like she needed a vacation from me too. What I don't remember is whether I even asked her about the trip. I was so self-absorbed in my own teenaged dramas, that I hardly remember any stories from her trip.

Then I stare at the photos of Nan as a younger woman, holding her granddaughter, cooing over me. It wouldn't be wrong to say that whatever light I stole from my mother's eyes seemed to appear in Nan's eyes. There was some connection that Nan and I had that was undeniable.

I start removing the photos from the pockets so that I can organize them for scanning them. It will be a long project, but I will be glad to have done it. As I begin pulling them out, I notice her handwriting on the backs of a few of them. Years, names, that sort of thing. I curse as I rip a photo of her and Nan, but a little tape on the back seems to fix it.

In one pocket, I discover a photo behind a photo. It's stuck to the back of the photo in front of it, and I peel it away as carefully as I can.

My mobile distracts me, the way mobile phones do.

"Friday night. Drinking alone. R U?"

It's Felicity. She's been loving life in New York this week. Her sister is hardly ever home, because like everyone else in New York, she needs to work her ass off to make rent. That means Fee gets to hang in her place in Brooklyn, where she's got a workbench set up already. Her new client loves her jewelry, and Fee's got a couple commissions to make for her. And Benjamin was right. Fee quadrupled her prices, and the woman didn't blink.

But I'm worried about her. Every text I get from her involves shopping, drinking, or some new guy. And she hasn't even been there a full week yet. I've seen this pattern in her before. It's almost an involuntary drive to consume, whether it's clothes, alcohol, or sex. On one hand, she seems happier than ever, but on the other, I worry about the consequences down the road.

"Time to talk?" I text.

No response, so I try calling her. She picks up, and she's already slurring her words. Keep in mind, this can happen after about a teaspoon of alcohol, considering she weighs about 99 pounds. Which is part of the problem.

"Where's Suze tonight?" I ask. Her sister is the more level-headed of the two, and I'm hoping she'll be home soon.

"She's went out with her work friends in Manhattan. I told her I'm hanging in tonight. Trey said he might stop by on his way home from work," she explains.

"The booty call guy?" I ask.

"Yea, he's really sweet," she says.

"You'd be proud of me, Fee. I actually ordered a salad along with my pizza tonight. What'd you have for dinner?"

"What time is it? Is it dinner time already?" she asks.

It is nine o'clock. I know New Yorkers eat later, but this is classic Fee, forgetting to eat, which only magnifies the drinking.

"Oh, I just got a text from Trey. He's out front. Would I be a terrible friend if I ditched you now?"

"No, I get it, but Fee?"

"Yeah?"

"Be careful, okay?"

Spike and I turn back to the photo album. I look at the two photos I had almost peeled apart. The top one looks like an acting headshot. I can't tell if it was her press photo, or if she was in costume for a show. It was a cute flirty shirt that looked like it might have been from the romance that she starred in before I was born. It was a four-series rom-com called *Home Away from Home* and I must have watched it dozens of times. In it, an American actress (my mom) goes on vacation and explores the London theatre scene, where she is spotted by a famed director who gets her invited to auditions, but she has to impersonate a British person in order to get roles, which leads to all kinds of funny awkward moments, in which the famed director begins to fall for her, and in the end, she gets a role where she's supposed to be an American, and the critics are so impressed by her American accent. It's a silly plot, but I loved to see my mother on the screen.

I finally finesse the bottom photo off. Part of it is stuck to the back of the other photo, leaving a big white splotch on the middle of photo. It's my mom posing with one of her handsome beaus. They really are a striking couple, whoever he is. I stare at him for a few moments. He looks familiar, but I never could keep her guys straight.

I move on to the next photo, but then I pause. I begin to wonder why she hid this photo under the other photo. That little mystery compels me to get up off Vittsjö, despite how cozy I feel under the throw blanket. This triggers Spike into a fit of twitching and readjusting his position. Then he hops down in search of food. He recovered from the baked beans incident, but ever since, is eating through almost a whole head of lettuce every day. If a rabbit can look annoyed, he does. He's clearly pissed off that the lettuce leaves in his dish are limp. Like a dutiful rabbit mom, I head to the fridge, wash some new leaves, and before I can even put them in the bowl, Spike has his teeth, in all their underbite glory, attached to them.

While Spike munches, I'm looking for a razor blade, which I keep a stock of in the store for scraping off residues from stickers and other unidentified deposits that can be found on second-hand items that I'd rather not think about. I almost never go into the store past eight o'clock. Even though it's my own store, there's something creepy about being in an antique shop all alone at night. Despite the act of bravery I put on for Benjamin, I think what scares me most is the dolls. It's impossible not to imagine them coming to life and slashing me with the very razor blade I am seeking. Or possibly one of the pocket-knives, vintage woodworking tools, silver kitchen knives, or unfathomable antique medical devices that are littered throughout the displays. I slink into the store, grab a pack of razor blades, take one longing look at the Victorian chaise, trip over that god-damned ripped carpeting for about the thousandth time, and lock up again before the dolls can get me.

Spike is back on the sofa waiting for me. My heart is still pounding. Much as I love him, we both know he won't be an effective deterrent to the evil dolls below us. I give him a nuzzle anyway. He responds by giving himself a bath. It's clear he could give a shit about the possessed dolls.

As for the next development in my exciting Friday night alone, I can only say it must be fate that is guiding me. I gently scrape off the stuck bit of photograph, and gasp when it finally falls free. It fits perfectly into the photograph like a puzzle piece and finishes out my mom's torso. I can't believe my eyes. I rub them and bring the photo closer to my face. I crinkle my nose like a middle-aged person who needs reading glasses. And there it is, before my eyes.

It's the sapphire necklace.

It's a little wrinkled and buckled from being stuck to the other photo. But there is no mistaking the deep blue, the almond-shaped setting, and the bar of diamonds on either side. And even despite the photo being in sad shape, my mother looks stunning in the necklace.

And happy. She's leaning into the man in a way I didn't typically see with other men she knew. Her eyes had their shine and she looked so full of life and love.

The man was well-dressed. He had pulled her to him with his right arm, leaned in toward her, and his smile looked genuine too.

Could this be the philandering aristocrat that Benjamin told me about? The one who commissioned the necklace from Benjamin's dad?

I start googling how to restore photographs and realize it's complicated. I decide to carefully stow it in a plastic baggie for now.

By now it's getting late, and a Friday night alone isn't a Friday night alone without a bowl of ice cream. I settle down with my favorite flavor, mint chip of course, and watch some mindless TV. Benjamin implored me to catch up on *The Secrets of Isis*, a little-remembered superhero series where an ordinary schoolteacher turns into an Egyptian Goddess to solve the crisis of the episode. Two episodes in, I'm in agreement with Benj that it should be the next movie remake. It's terrible of course, but I love it.

I drift off before midnight, dreaming of morphing into Queen Victoria and lounging on chaises while ordering my armies around, jewels dangling off of every finger. The people are rebelling against me, and I am hiding my jewels and gold in the lining of my bustier. A courtier is fanning me, but I'm hot as hell because my gowns are made of heavy wool and my corset is cutting off my circulation. A painter is trying to paint my portrait, but I insist he leaves lest he paint me in this bothered condition. I begin to realize I'm a true royal bitch when the dream begins to fade.

Two in the morning, and my fire alarm is blaring. No, it's just my phone. Spike is cuddled near my chin.

"Hi babe, just calling to say goodnight."

"Mmm," I mutter.

"Oh, shit, it's late there, isn't it?"

I can't tell if Benjamin is giving me payback for waking him at five in the morning, or if he honestly forgot it is three hours later here.

I drift back off to sleep, this time with happier dreams of Victorian chaises, where I am doing royally unspeakable things with a certain aquamarine-eyed courtier that I wonder if any person in Victorian times ever imagined having the freedom to do.

Chapter 17

"Nothing's truer than a child's storybook."

We have a lot of early editions of books in the store, including a section of children's books from the 1950's and 1960's, which is popular with grandparents, hoping their grandchildren will want to relive the same stories they enjoyed when they were little. Many of these old stories have been redesigned for today's kids. And when I say redesigned, I say this euphemistically. What I really mean is that they've been chopped in half – or more – for today's short attention span. The original Curious George Flies a Kite book is 80 pages long! What child – or what tired overworked parent – has the patience for an 80 page book about a mischievous monkey?

I had recently purchased an original 1960 printing of Are You My Mother, the one where that bird hatches while his mother is away getting food, and he proceeds to look for her, asking every car, boat, and plane whether they are his mother. It clocks in at an impressive 64 pages, and as far as I know, this one has stood the test of time. The new editions haven't been cut at all, and the simple P.D. Eastman illustrations still have a way of speaking to children. I set it up behind my locked display case and posted it on eBay too.

This morning I smile at P.D. Eastman book as I pass it. My own mother was a mystery to me in many ways, as I discovered in her photo albums last night. Makes me wish

I could go back in time and ask her a few things.

It's an unusually warm day for January, so Geena and I take a coffee break and sit on two matching wrought iron stools outside the shop taking in some sun. Each of these stools weighs at least a metric tonne, and I'm hoping they sell soon so that I don't have to keep moving them around. But for today, they are the perfect spot to take a load off.

Geena nearly falls off her stool when I show her the photograph from last night, the stool tipping precariously sideways as she is lurching forward.

"I can't believe it. I can't believe it after all these years. Incredible!" she says, centering herself on the stool again.

"Geena, you're killing me. What's so incredible that you can't even balance on that two-ton stool?"

She composes herself and steps carefully off the stool. She backs up onto the sidewalk, with her back to the street and looks critically at me. Then looks critically at the picture, and then back at me.

"I don't want to say this and find out I'm wrong, but it's simply uncanny," she says.

I start to break out in a sweat, even though it's only barely warm enough to be sitting outside. I get a sense that something dramatic is happening, yet I still feel sheltered in the comfort of ignorance. If I can just stay in my state of ignorance, everything will be okay.

"Would you just tell me, already?" I say. But I think I already know what she is going to say.

"It's gotta be him, Grace. It's where you get your brow, your eyes, your cheekbones, maybe even your jawline. It's remarkable." She tempers her enthusiasm when she sees the shell-shocked look on my face.

I have never spent an undue amount of time wondering who my father might be. My mother and Nan were all the family I needed, and they instilled in me a self-reliance in which I never questioned if anyone was missing from my life. When I was little, my mother gave me vague answers about my father being a good person who just didn't happen to live with us. As I got older, the answers stayed just as vague. And when I was old enough to understand the revolving door of boyfriends in her life, and how they seemed interchangeable with one another, I figured some anonymous man out there was the unwitting sperm donor who made up the other half of my DNA, but he was about as relevant to my life as the rest of the men she dated.

Still, I can't help feeling the pull of biology. I take the photo back from Geena as she searches her pocket for something. She pulls out four blank price tags and uses them to frame the man's face, covering up his hair, so that all I can see is his face. And damn if she's not right. I'm staring into my own face in that picture. It's pretty high on the creepy scale. Maybe not as high as the killer dolls in the basement, but still up there.

"Did my mom ever tell you anything about him?" I ask her.

"No, she kept it a secret from everyone. Never told your grandmother, not her girlfriends, no one," Geena confirms. "But I always suspected she felt something for your father, given how hard she loved you. She was a complicated woman, your mom. Seemed like she never felt entirely happy unless she had a boyfriend to go out with, yet she broke up with them left and right, even the really nice ones. She had that independent streak that trumped everything else."

We sit in silence for a few minutes. We both zipper

our coats up under our chins. Maybe it is colder out here than we first thought.

"Too bad the photo is ripped so badly," Geena says. I had left the remnant that shows the necklace in my apartment.

"I'm just lucky it wasn't their faces. It was stuck to a photo in the same album, and this was the best I could do, even with my trusty razor blade," I say.

"So, the big question. What next? Will you try to find out who he is?" Geena asks.

In my mind this is not the only big question. My mind is spinning with them. Is my father really the philandering aristocrat? How in the world did my mother meet him? Did he give custom-designed jewelry to all of his mistresses? And did his synthetic sapphire really get swapped with Princess Diana's one-of-a-kind authentic sapphire? For the first time in my life, I have more than a passing curiosity about my father. Now I want to get to the bottom of what in the world is going on, and what I'm supposed to do about the missing sapphire. Call the police? Call my new father? Tell Benjamin? But for now, I'm keeping all that to myself.

"I guess maybe I should try to at least find out who he is, but no, I can't imagine approaching some 60-year old man and saying, 'are you my father'?" I answer.

We head back into the store as some customers arrive. The woman is looking for a Pfaltzgraff creamer to match the one in a set she's had since the dawn of time. And when I say the dawn of time, I say this literally. This woman must be 102 years old if she is a day.

"I'm 103, did you know that?" she says, almost reading my mind. Then again, most of my customers who are over the age of 90 love to tell me how old they are. They wear it like a badge. Hell, I will too, if I make it that long.

But some days, like today, I feel like I am missing out on my finest years spending them in the company of so many old folks. No offense to Geena. She's old too, but so young at heart that I feel like I can tell her anything.

In a minor miracle, I do have the exact creamer that this impressively spry centenarian wants, and she purchases a set of mugs too.

"You Nancy's daughter?" she asks.

"Her granddaughter," I say, suddenly worried that I'm turning into an old person too.

"Oh, sorry, how ridiculous of me. I forget how old I am sometimes. Of course, you're too young to be her daughter. I wanted to compliment you on the store. I thought no one could get the kind of merchandise that Nancy did, and keep the displays looking so fresh, but I was wrong. I'm always impressed when I come in."

"She taught me well," I say with a grin.

"And you're gorgeous too," she says, patting my hand as I give her the receipt.

"Thank you," I say, and try to drink in the compliment like Geena told me.

Geena winks at me in a sign of support. She has a hair appointment, but offers to come back if I want to talk more about the photo of my alleged father. But there's too much that I can't share with her yet, and we leave it at that.

"Hey gorgeous," comes a text from Benjamin.

I smile. Two gorgeouses in a row. It seems like the world is supporting me today, on this day that I discover I may have a father after all.

"Hey handsome," I say. Unimaginative, but sometimes the truth is good enough.

Benjamin: I miss seeing you. Facetime over dinner 2nite?

Me: Chinese takeout?

Benjamin: Perfect

Me: Okay if I get oyster sauce? You can't be allergic through Facetime, can you?

Benjamin: Don't know. Never made out with anyone through Facetime before.

Me: You think you're going to get lucky tonight?

Benjamin: A man can always dream.

Chapter 18

"A chocolate a day keeps the stress away."

Nan would always keep a bowl of Tootsie Rolls at the counter in the store, and would push them on people like they were a delicacy not to be missed. She'd always have a few in her pocket. And if I was ever upset about anything, she would see Tootsie Rolls as the salve. Like a British person would use a cup of tea as the cure-all, Nan would bring out the Tootsie Rolls.

I never told her this, but I don't actually like Tootsie Rolls. What is their flavor, after all? Is it really chocolate? Is it taffy? I'm not a fan of the in-between. I'd prefer it to be one or the other. And given how long they sit in the candy dish uneaten, I think I'm not alone in this. Hershey Kisses? They disappear from the candy dish before noon. A bag of Tootsie Rolls can last the whole month. Despite this, I feel a responsibility for keeping the Tootsie Roll alive, for Nan's sake. So I usually keep a bowl of the wrapped treats by the cash register to this day.

The one exception I make is for Halloween. Let's face it, kids do not want Tootsie Rolls for Halloween, much as Nan insisted on giving them out every year. I gave out Tootsie Rolls one more year after she died, but then upgraded to Twix, Twizzlers, Skittles, Snickers, you name it. Anything but the lowly Tootsie Roll. Nan might never forgive me when we meet again, but the kids have loved the change.

The store is a fairly big draw every October. We clear out most of the front show room of our regular wares and set up a mini-haunted house for the neighborhood kids. And more and more, kids from other neighborhoods come too. When I was young, my Halloween was like most kids' Christmas. Hands-down, my favorite day of the year.

We have no shortage of Halloween decorations that I've picked up at garage sales, estate sales, and trash piles over the years. The more dilapidated the better. Then, of course as I've mentioned before, there are the dolls. You cannot buy dolls this scary in your average Halloween store. If I were a believer, I would think a few of them are actually haunted by spirits past. The best are the dolls with porcelain heads where the paint is chipping off. When they're in poor condition, they are not worth much money for resale, but they're invaluable for fright night. The Germans of the late 1800's seemed to have cornered the market on creepy dolls. At the time they were praised and coveted for their realism, especially of their skin tone. The rarer models of Kestner and Kling dolls still go for some money if you can find the right collector, but the more common dolls aren't worth much, and are well worth the looks of glee or fright on the faces of our visitors each year.

I'm thinking about Halloween and spooky creatures and decide to darken my eye makeup along the lines of a vampiress. Not too dark, or I'll look like a corpse on Facetime, but just enough to give me a bad-girl edge. I find a black blouse with the kind of plunging neckline that I know Benjamin will go for and pull some of my hair up into a messy bun. I take Geena's words to heart and tell myself I'm gorgeous as I finish my lipstick.

The doorbell rings. It's the takeout. My favorite Chinese restaurant includes a fresh quartered orange with every delivery, along with free fortune cookies and an ample supply of duck sauce packets. The man who delivers my dinner must deliver to so many addresses that he can't keep them straight, but tonight he seems to remember me. We chat about the unseasonably warm weather, and he smiles when I hand him three Tootsie Rolls with his tip. I always do this. It's a Nan thing that I've adopted.

About five minutes into our date, I realize that all my preparation in front of the mirror was for naught. Benjamin insists we eat with chopsticks, especially because he has no other utensils in his hotel room. Not only am I making a mess of my Kung Pao Chicken, smearing my lipstick, and slopping sauce on my face, but he's not even looking at me because he is so intent on eating noodle soup. I can hear his soup splashing onto his cheeks. His phone is tilted, so all I can see is the bottom half of his face.

We finally clean ourselves up and look up from our meals in a kind of relief.

"Next time, cameras off for the eating part, okay?" I say.

"Deal. Hey, fabulous shirt. Just how far down does it, uh, …"

"Mind out of the gutter, Benj."

"Oh yeah, right, of course. But can I say you are a sight for sore eyes? I'm in the land of plastic out here. Plastic trees, plastic landmarks, plastic people. Is anything real in Las Vegas?"

"Not that I know of. Except maybe your casino debt, you know?"

"Tomorrow I fly into New York City. I got a hotel room in mid-town from Friday to Monday. Can you come up and see me? It's not far, is it?"

As much as I would love to visit his hotel room, I have no one to cover the store. Scratch that excuse. Truth be told, Geena would probably be happy to cover it for me. But the reality is, I still haven't recovered from my failures in New York. Laid off from two entry level copywriting jobs in two different marketing agencies within the space of one year. And dumped by a man who was twice my age for a woman who was half my weight, leaving me with nowhere to live that was affordable on my bakery assistant's salary.

I make excuses and hear the disappointment in his voice.

"Listen, I heard from your best mates Jeremy and Ian."

"Wait, what? Why didn't you tell me sooner? Did they call your fake voicemail?"

"Yes, Jeremy left three voicemails in one day. On the last one, he says he'd even come to my store in Miami. He's totally blowing his cover of an average bloke shopping for his wife. He's desperate to find the sapphire."

"But who is he?"

"Still dunno. I finally told my father about him. He has a right to know that I'm not the only one looking for the sapphire. He's going to look into it on his end, for what that's worth."

This is not what I expected. I truly thought that Jeremy had somehow cracked my safe and stolen the necklace. If not Jeremy, then who?

Just then, Spike darts out from around the corner, afraid of something. Most times rabbits are afraid of something, it's something of their own making. This time, Spike is sitting on the pile of photos that I had left on the sofa the previous night, and has succeeded in scattering them across the sofa and the floor. I think maybe he's telling me something about the photos, so I decide to share some of my news with Benjamin.

"I've uncovered another mystery today, too," I begin, "In my mom's photo albums."

"Let me hear it. You and I, we could be a detective team. What is it, love?"

I show him the photo.

"Is that your Mum then? Pretty, she is – not as pretty as you though. And who's the bloke? He looks familiar somehow. Hold it steady. Yea, I'm sure I've seen that fellow somewhere. He'd be older now, 'course, but definitely looks familiar. Is he famous or something?"

"I don't know who he is, but I think I know why he looks familiar to you. Zoom in on just his face, and see if you see what I mean." I snap a photo of the photo and text it to Benjamin.

"Well, if I had to say," he mutters, as he's looking at his mobile, "I'd say he looks like… oh bloody hell, that's gotta be your father, right? He looks just like you, Grace!"

"Mmm-hmm," I say.

I desperately want to ask Benjamin to show the photo to his dad, to verify that it is the noble dude who commissioned the necklace for my mom. But how do I ask him without revealing that I've seen the necklace? Or without revealing that my mother was wearing the necklace in this photo?

"Well that must come as a shock. How're you feeling about it?"

"Better now, that I'm talking to you."

"You think you'll try to find him?"

"I don't know, but fact is, I'm really tired of thinking about it today, and would love to talk about something else, to get my mind off it."

"Can we talk about your blouse again?" Benjamin says.

I tilt the camera and show him just how low it goes. And I discover that my British beau cannot only impersonate an American, but has the perfect accent for the Italian lover, the French romancer, and the Spanish seduction artist. Lovemaking over the phone turns out to be miles better than attempting to eat Chinese food over the phone. I'm beginning to think a long-distance relationship may be possible after all.

∞∞∞

For the second night this week, my phone rings at 2am. Must be Benjamin again.

"I'm crazy over you, Benj, and you rock phone sex like I didn't even know was possible, but we need to have a heart-to-heart about time zones," I say.

"Sorry to wake you, love, but this is important. The photo. It finally came to me."

"You only just got my text?"

"No, it finally came to me why I recognized the man. It's not just because he so obviously looks like you. It's because he's one of our clients. None other than the philandering aristocrat I told you about!"

"You mean the cheating married son of a bitch who gave my mom the sapphire necklace?"

"Yes, but I wouldn't want to call him a son of a bitch now that I know he's your father. And in reality, I've met him at our retail store, and he seems pretty decent."

"Wait, you're not kidding me? You think it's him?" It is what I had guessed, but Benj identifying him made it even more real. The pieces of the puzzle are falling into place.

"I don't think it. I know it. I know he is the philandering aristocrat. And I even know his title. He is officially the 9th Earl of Heathwood. His name is Harry Alexander George Britton. I'm looking at him on Wikipedia right now. This is proof that I am not shitting you Grace."

"Then I would prefer it if you would call me *Lady Grace*," I say.

"How can you be joking at a time like this?" he says.

"I don't know. I'm flipping out inside, to tell the truth. I've finally after all these years discovered a ripped up photo of the man who is probably my father, and then, I find out he's British royalty?

"Nobility, baby, not royalty."

"Nobility, royalty, whatever. Your country is weird."

"Trust me, you don't want to be related to royalty! Talk about a fucked up family."

"So nobility's better?"

"Marginally."

"Okay, so yes, I'm freaking out inside. But honestly? While I'm talking to you, it feels like everything is okay."

"I know the feeling, Lady Grace."

Chapter 19

"Never judge a woman by her hat pin."

*T*his aphorism of Nan's made no sense at all, which is why she liked it. She'd trot it out whenever she feared I was judging another person, criticizing someone, or just getting too high-minded. She was a true egalitarian and if I learned nothing else from her, she wanted me to learn this. If she hadn't quite managed to teach it to her fashion-conscious, social-climbing daughter, she was determined that her granddaughter understand it. The hat pin bit inevitably led to us talking about silly hats we'd gotten in the shop, or how sadistic and dangerous hat pins were as a method of keeping a hat on your head. She had figured out that her lessons on egalitarianism were best learned while I was joking with her about weird Victorian hat-wearing customs than sitting around a dinner table getting lectured.

Today I know that Nan, may she rest in ever loving peace, would be turning over in her grave, if she hadn't been cremated that is, at my blue-bloodedness. I'm Nobility! I'm an Aristocrat! How patrician I feel today, I think to myself, as I open up the store. Makes me wonder if that's why my mom never revealed who my father was. She knew her own mother would be horrified that she was, let's just say, *fraternizing* with an honest-to-goodness Earl!

I can already tell it's going to be a weird day. Spike

would not get out of bed this morning, despite my bribing him with a handful of fresh organic shredded carrots. I trip over the carpet remnant yet again, this time jamming my toes so badly I'm sure I've broken one of them. And I'm tired as a dog, after my late night session with Benjamin and the mental turmoil of finding out my dad is a two-timing Earl.

Benjamin is on a flight with two stops back to the east coast, so our voice calls are put on hold, and considering their X-rated nature, it's probably for the best. But I'm still getting scintillating texts from him every hour on the hour. He's tireless. And I love it.

Apart from that, I'm hiding out on my laptop hoping no one comes into the store. I've got some research to do. I read that my father is indeed the 9th Earl of Heathwood. He's 64 years old and has been divorced for the last 25 years. I do the math and work out that he must have been 34 when he was with my mother and seven years into his doomed marriage. The seven year itch, and it looks like he scratched it. He honestly has three first names. It makes me wonder, did my mom refer to him as Harry Alexander George, or just Harry?

What's interesting to me is that he seems like a regular person. Like a person with a job, as opposed to Lord Grantham padding around the Downton Abbey mansion and looking down his nose at the underlings while at the end of each episode being proven to have more heart than you expected.

My father's life doesn't appear to be all that aristocratic, when it comes right down to it. He's a small-time director of films and television shows, excuse me, *programmes*. And this may be the final piece of the puzzle. I look at his TV credits, and I almost have a heart attack when I see that he directed *Home Away from Home.* Yep, the same rom-com I watched over and over again, not knowing that my own father was the director. Or that he was having an affair with the lead actress, my mother.

How did my mother let me watch that show? It must have brought back so many memories for her. Whether they were good or bad, I didn't know. She always acted happy that I liked the show and laughed at all the appropriate spots. It fascinated me to watch a younger version of my mother in action on the screen. She looked so beautiful and young, and I couldn't believe all the casting agents in the world didn't hire her on the spot. But she would downplay it, and claim she wasn't good enough for the big time.

There's no way in hell she didn't resent me for derailing her acting career. Did she resent the Earl too, for knocking her up in the first place? Did she even tell the Earl about me?

I close the store for an hour and go back up to my apartment to dig through more of my mom's boxes. I don't know what I'm looking for. More photos of my father? Some clue that my mom may have hidden for me to find? Some memorabilia from the *Home Away from Home* show? News clippings that she might have saved?

I hit pay dirt when I find a small stack of air mail letters, the old-fashioned kind on special blue paper. They were the self-mailing sort that required no envelope. There is no signature and no return address on any of them, but the postmark is the United Kingdom. I'm certain it's him. And when I say I'm certain, I do not say it literally. With my mom's proclivities, I know these love letters could be from practically anyone.

But one thing I know: after I start reading the letters, I

want it to be him. This guy was clearly falling in love with my mother, all, it appeared, by airmail.

Dearest Lily,

Your letter had me in stitches, and I could almost hear your delightful laughter in my head when your customer mistook you for Winona Rider. Who knew that selling cosmetics at Macy's could result in such a rich array of stories? But then again, I think you bring that kind of energy and light with you wherever you go.

Congratulations for your role in "Boy Meets World!" I knew you could do it! The more auditions you attend, the more you will be offered roles. Any good director will notice you in a heartbeat. Your acting instincts are spot on, and I'm not just saying that because I am over the moon about you. When does filming begin? I wish there were some way for me to see the American programmes here.

You know I will ask you, because I ask you every time, but won't you consider coming back to London, if not to see me, then for an audition? My next television series looks promising. *The Adder's Tale*. The writer's got natural talent for creating suspense. The cliff hangers and the plot twists are completely unpredictable, if we can get the set and lighting just right. And if we have the right cast. The heroine – I can't think of anyone more perfect than you for the role.

I eagerly await your next letter.

Love and kisses and more,

me

He clearly wanted more from the relationship and in the next letter, he proposed a rendezvous in Paris, a meet-up in the U.S., or anything she wanted. It was unclear whether she ever agreed. In one letter, he shed some light on his marriage, a modern-day arranged marriage with the daughter of an influential family, also considered nobility. He professed that the marriage was loveless and that my mother was the only person in his life who wasn't constantly asking him to measure up to a preconceived notion of what an Earl in the modern century was supposed to do and be. It might make an "uncomfortable splash" in the tabloids, but he would leave his wife for her.

I would guess that my mother responded with letters of her own. I have no way of knowing for sure whether she mentioned me, but one thing is clear: In none of the letters does he refer to me. He doesn't even appear to realize that my mother has a daughter at all. Nor does he refer to his own children. It's almost as if he's living in an alternate reality in which motherhood and fatherhood are not really consequential. Yet the letters, in their love-struck innocence, are charming in their own way. Maybe he realized that life with her was fantasy talk. Maybe they both did.

I finish reading the letters and feel that I have learned at least a little more about my father. But there is not much else. My mother wasn't much of a sentimentalist, and judging from the gaps in the dates, it appears she saved only ten letters out of what may have been many more. I am lucky these ten letters even made the cut.

But what the letters do show me was a level of respect and decency that I hadn't expected. True, he was cheating on his wife, but to know my mother was loved by someone—that particular someone who happened to be my father—is something that I had never expected to learn.

I had always thought fathers were for other kids, not me. And now, to learn that my father was sending letters to our apartment over the course of several years made me realize how close to having a father I actually was. If only she had chosen to let him in.

By now my emotions are getting the better of me, and I'm feeling hurt, resentful, and confused. I don't understand why my mother would hide the father of her only child. He seemed to love her and was willing to take any small part of her attention that she was willing to give. Could she not at least have introduced us?

These thoughts roll around in my head and culminate into one intense feeling. The feeling of being alone. Isolated. Abandoned.

But as I hit bottom, a new realization slowly dawns on me. Maybe I am not as alone as I think. I have an idea and I go back to Wikipedia. Thanks to the wonders of the paparazzi and the world wide web, I learn that I am not alone in this world at all. I now have, and have had for three decades, unbeknownst to me, four half-siblings. I don't know why it never occurred to me that my until-now-anonymous father may have sired other human beings, but it hadn't. What's more, I'm not the only illegitimate child of the philandering Earl. One of my half-brothers was born before the Earl's arranged marriage to his wife, but he never married that woman. Basically, my family tree has just grown from the Charlie Brown Christmas Tree into the Rockefeller Center holiday tree.

∞ ∞ ∞

"Fee, you're never gonna believe this," I say.

"Hang on, I'm just checking out," she says.

By the way her voice is fading in and out, I can tell she's holding her cell phone hands-free, with it squeezed between her shoulder and her ear as she shops.

"Are Uggs still in?" she asks. "I just got two new pair. Are they too frumpy? Shit, maybe I should return them. I'm gonna return them and get, I don't know, do you think it would be kinda sexy to wear cowboy boots? I think there's something kind of *rebel* about them, don't you?"

"Maybe just get one pair instead of two? You did say your credit card was imploding," I say. I hate to feel like a school marm scolding her, but I can tell she's spiraling out of control.

"I'll get two and you can borrow one next time we go out. But no more drinking at Puke's Tavern, Grace. We can do so much better than Puke's. The bars here are so classy, and so is the clientele. Boy, I'd love to live here, wouldn't you?"

She seems to have completely forgotten that I already tried living in New York. In fact, she seems to be wrapped up so completely in the city, that I can tell she's not even listening to me. New York can do that to people. It's completely absorbing in all its frenetic energy. I decide not to tell her my news yet. I'll wait until she comes home.

"Suze is trying to convince me to make the move. It's really tempting. What do you think, shouldn't everyone live in New York, at least for a while?" she says. "I just adore this place! I mean, what are we waiting for, Grace? Let's get off our butts and live a little!"

I sigh and wrap up the call as I hear her credit card shifting into warp speed. Maybe, I think as I read about my long-lost relatives, her advice isn't half bad.

Chapter 20

"Genetics: can't deny 'em, can't defy 'em."

Nan and I used to like to play our own secret game with the customers milling about the store. We would walk the floors too, trying to be of service to the customers, or ostensibly dusting or rearranging some merchandise. But what we were really doing was attempting to match the customers with the old portraits of unknown subjects hanging about the store for sale. One point for each face that was similar; two points if both their face and their clothing style matched. Whoever was the first to call it won the points. We could have used an impartial judge, because more often than not, we couldn't agree on whether or not there really was a resemblance. It was usually me who objected. But how else was I to win any points at all? Nan had most of the portraits memorized, if they'd sat unsold in the store long enough, and invariably a big smile would spread across her face when a new customer arrived. I could tell she was sizing up which portrait was the best match.

After Nan passed away, the portraits returned to what they had always been to me: creepy. I tried for a few months to keep the spirit of the game alive, and would scan customers for facial features that matched the dour-looking 19th century woman with the bonnet, or the stern woman in funereal clothing looking young yet old, possibly widowed at a young age, or even the youngish woman in the bodice with the severe

look on her face. But instead of finding a silly familial resem-
blance, I just missed Nan and felt creeped out by the spirits of
these Victorian era portrait subjects in my space. I mean, give
a girl a break, would it have been too much to smile?

I am worried that Felicity may be headed off the deep end, but her final words stick with me. Isn't it time to live a little? The store isn't busy in January. I can easily get someone to manage it. Why sit on my butt researching my family tree in the never-ending land of cyberspace when I could get on a plane and go meet them? Isn't 31 years long enough to wait?

I start looking at flights to London. Then I start cross-referencing the cost of the tickets with my current bank balance. The comparison is not favorable. I'd better sell something big in the store if I want to afford this.

By divine intervention, my mobile rings just that moment. The number looks familiar, but it's not coming up as one of my contacts. But in my business, it could be a potential customer, buyer, trader, or vendor, so I pick it up.

"Hello, luv, is this Grace?" A British accent, familiar voice. "It's Jeremy, the fellow who was looking for a necklace for his wife?"

Shit, I think, I nearly forgot about the necklace! I guess he got tired of leaving messages on Benjamin's fake voice-mail.

"Any luck on the necklace?" I play along, stalling for time. Benjamin still hasn't figured out who these guys are, and it scares me a little how persistent Jeremy is. How does he know about the necklace and why does he want it so badly?

"No luck, and I'm beginning to think you know why. Grace, we need to talk."

I can't tell if there's a menacing undertone to his

voice, but he definitely sounds serious. I agree to meet him and Ian at a coffee shop that afternoon. He's making me a little nervous, so I want to be sure to pick a public place that's busier than my sleepy store.

I think of texting Benjamin about this new development, but I really want to solve this on my own. I think of how impressed he will be if he steps off his flight, and I tell him who Jeremy and Ian are and why they are so intent on finding the same necklace.

I suggest to Jeremy that we meet at Carla's Cuppa. I know Carla from many years of buying her coffee for Nan when I was young, and now being a regular myself. She was one of my favorites in Nan's Sisterhood. Like all of Nan's friends, Carla had a straightforwardness that I appreciated, and in this regard, Carla went above and beyond. Brash, brassy, brusque, brazen, and in my eyes, brilliant. All the good "br" words bundled up in one fiery woman. And there was no one more loyal to her friends than Carla.

She serves up a straight black coffee that could compete with any meth or coke being sold on the streets. She's reluctantly updated her coffee menu over the years to offer all the high-end coffee drinks too, but today feels like a day for the straight caffeine hit.

I've briefed Carla that she needs to keep an eye on me, and if I signal her that something is fishy, she'll intervene. I have full faith in her ability to back me up. Carla is someone that you don't want to mess with. As part of Nan's Sisterhood, these women always had each other's backs, and by extension they've got mine, too. It's just one of the many ways that my Nan lives on, and I smile up to her in the sky, where heaven is supposed to be, just in case she's watching. And I think she must be, because at that moment, a bolt of January sunshine opens up in the sky, shining directly into my eye. I'm still seeing spots when I arrive at Carla's Cuppa.

I step through the doors and I am feeling a little nervous. Do Jeremy and Ian know that I had the necklace? What will they do if I tell them it's been stolen? Jeremy walks in and finds me seated in the corner table. He orders a coffee and purchases three of Carla's carrot muffins. How did he know they are my favorite? Ian arrives a few moments later and orders at the counter.

Jeremy looks at me with a sheepish smile. I stare down at my coffee, not knowing what to say.

"We haven't been entirely truthful with you, Grace," Jeremy begins.

"You can say that again," I say. I would prefer to say, "No shit, Sherlock," because how often do you get to say that to a real British person? But I do have some manners now and then.

"Let me start by introducing myself properly. I'm Jeremy Robinson, and this is Ian Walker. We are not shopping in antiques stores for our wives' birthdays. We work outside of London for the 9th Earl of Heathwood Harry Alexander George Britton, or in more common parlance, Earl H. Alex Britton, or even just Alex for short."

I nearly choke on my carrot muffin. What are the odds of hearing about this Earl two days in a row? It doesn't take a Master Mind to know that a major cosmic collision is happening in my world right now.

"On the Earl's request, we came to the U.S. in search of a particular necklace which was gifted to your mother some 31 years ago. We had learned of your mother's passing, may she rest in peace, and believed the necklace might be in your hands, or somewhere on the market in the U.S. The Earl has never regretted gifting your mother the necklace, but now that she has passed, he believes it rightly belongs to the Britton family, and he hoped to purchase it back for that reason," Jeremy explains.

I am still in shock, so to avoid responding, I take another large inelegant bite of my carrot muffin. A few crumbs spill down my top, and a hunk of the muffin breaks off and somehow lands in Jeremy's coffee. He fishes it out with a spoon and politely sets it on a saucer, acting completely unfazed.

"Ahem," Ian quietly says.

"Okay, to be fair," Jeremy concedes, "The Earl himself couldn't give a rat's arse about the necklace. It's his daughter, Isabella, who is so keen on recovering it."

"Is it real sapphire?" I ask, finally finding my voice.

"As I understand it," Jeremy explains, "It is what they call lab-created. So it's real sapphire, just not naturally found. This particular specimen is large – nearly 24 carats – flawless, clear, and stunning, at least according to the Earl's daughter, who heard it from the Earl's ex-wife, who has been wondering where the sapphire is ever since their divorce 25 years ago that left her with a cheap sapphire substitute."

Just then an espresso machine whirs into action, and I can't hear a word Jeremy is saying. Ian turns around to see what's happening behind the bar, where Carla is creating an intricate design with the steamed milk and looking over at Ian with what can only be described as a come-hither expression. It is not particularly becoming for Carla, because it is drawing attention to her triple chin, yet it appears to be working on Ian. He is transfixed and ogles her hips as she's bringing him the steaming mug.

No offense to my sixty-year-old friends, and in my

line of business, I have plenty of them, but it is somewhere between stomach-churning and full-out nauseating to watch the older generation flirting. I admit it, this is ageist, but, well, puh-leeease!

Carla sets down Ian's mug with a flourish, and I look at Ian's cappuccino in disbelief. As long as I have been coming to Carla's, I have never once heard the espresso machine being used. She has claimed for years that it is broken, and that besides, lattes are for wimps. "It's called a coffee shop," she typically explains. "Your choices are coffee or coffee."

Which is why the milky design on Ian's cappuccino is blowing my mind. It's a work of art from a woman who might kick your ass if you ask for soy milk. It's a multi-petaled flower in perfect symmetry. Jeremy and I are now both staring at it, because it's excruciating to witness Ian's doe eyes connecting with Carla's. The pattern in the milk is diffusing, and right before our eyes, it begins to take on the shape of a, no, this can't be, I tell myself, but it begins to morph into a defining feature of the human male anatomy, complete with two anatomically correct playthings.

"Uh, excuse me, I need to take this call," Jeremy and I say in unison. We each play-act that our phones are ringing and scamper off to opposite corners of the shop. I check my phone and see a few messages from Benjamin have come in. He's still en route.

Benjamin: Miniature vodkas rule!

Me: Drinking already?

Benjamin: Had to try a Bloody Mary, no? When in America, do as the Americans do, right?

Me: No real Americans drink Bloody Mary's!

Benjamin: No wonder! They taste like shiite!

Me: Eye roll

Benjamin: Who's idea was it to put Worcestershire sauce in a breakfast drink anyway?

Me: Dr. Poison?

Benjamin: I don't even understand the tomato juice.

Me: IKR? Tomatoes are for spaghetti sauce.

I look up and Jeremy is still nervously scrolling through his phone, and if my eyes don't deceive me, Carla is about ready to sit in Ian's lap when a group of four enter the store. Carla strokes Ian's shoulder and backs away like they're lovers being separated by an invisible cosmic force.

Benjamin: Gotta tell you something

Me: Go ahead, shoot!

Benjamin: Shoot?

Me: Shoot, like "go ahead, tell me"

Benjamin: You're weird.

Me: That's what you had to tell me?

Benjamin: No, silly! I've got a lead on the sapphire necklace. Someone in New York.

Me: Really?

Benjamin: Really! I'll call you when I can talk privately.

Me: Ooo, I like it when we talk privately

Benjamin: Now whose mind is in the gutter?

Me: Touché

Benjamin: Heart emoji, fire emoji

Me: Kiss emoji

Benjamin: Someone needs to invent X-rated emojis

It seems safe to return to the table. Carla is busy serving the other guests, and Ian has nearly returned to his steady state.

"Ahem, so where were we?" Jeremy begins, giving Ian a raised eyebrow. "We work for the Earl of Heathwood, and we are trying to recover the sapphire necklace that he had gifted your mother many years ago. As you can guess, we have been unsuccessful in finding the necklace for the Earl's demanding—excuse me—devoted daughter. But I believe we have found something better."

He pauses and waits for me to speak. I'm feeling annoyed that he's playing some kind of game with me, so I say nothing. It's like a game of chicken as to who will break the silence. I win.

"I believe we have found something that will make him far happier," Jeremy continues. "I think we have found his long-lost daughter."

I just look at Jeremy with a blank expression. I don't know how they figured this out, when I only just worked it out myself. I wasn't ready to share this news with anyone yet, let alone these two strangers. But then I look across the table, and both Jeremy and Ian are smiling at me in what I can only describe as a genuinely welcoming manner. They look like they are about to cry.

"I found a photograph and some love letters, and was starting to come to that conclusion myself," I say, cautiously. "How did you find out? Did my mother ever tell him about me?"

"No, the Earl never knew your mother even had a child until reading her obituary, and at that, never knew he was your father until the day before yesterday."

"So who told him?"

"We did," Jeremy says, with the tearful smile again. "When we came into your store last week, we were both immediately struck by the resemblance. It was undeniable. But we needed to find out more about you before presenting our theory to the Earl."

"So you spied on me?"

"No, not exactly. We only looked through public records. There was an article a few years back in the local newspaper about your store. In it, you mentioned growing up in a single parent household. And the date of your birth aligns with the time that your mother was in London filming the Earl's picture *Home Away from Home*. And there might also be the small matter of the chewing gum you discarded into a tissue before speaking with us. Ian's a right Sherlock Holmes for catching that."

"You did not test my DNA! Is that even legal?"

"Good question!" Jeremy says.

"Beats me," Ian adds. "But it indicated a 99.99% chance that he is your father, Grace. Surely you've wanted to have this question answered all your life, haven't you?"

"Who are you to guess what I've wanted all my life?" I say angrily.

"We only wanted you to know," says Ian quietly.

I can't keep up my indignity any longer and break down in tears. Me sobbing: Not a pretty sight. I don't cry daintily or quietly. It's massive involuntary sobs, sputtering, and gasping. Coupled with Carla's caffeine kicking in, the sobs come faster and more violently, and I'm shaking and quivering not unlike Spike.

"Yo! You leave her alone. No jackasses allowed in my store! Out, out! Or I call the cops!" Carla breaks in, battering Ian and Jeremy with a rolled up copy of *Rolling Stone* magazine. She pulls back Ian's chair, nearly tipping him on his bottom and grabs Jeremy by the coat sleeve. They look up at her in terror. Carla can do this to people.

I can't help loving Carla for protecting me over her new boyfriend Ian. But I'm worried she's shot to hell any chances of winning Ian over now.

"No, Carla!" I say, "It's fine, really! They're fine!" And the ridiculousness of the situation turns my sobs into laughter, and before we know what's happening, we're all laughing like we're long lost friends.

I agree to meet Jeremy again tomorrow once I've had time to come to terms with everything. He wants to tell me about the family, its history, my half-siblings, the works. And honestly, I am all ears, but just want to go home and think a little.

Ian and Carla are drifting closer to each other again, her outburst seeming to have intensified their attraction. But before a complete coupling ensues, the gentlemen extend an open-ended invitation for an all-expenses paid trip to London when I am ready. Bingo, my bank balance issue is solved.

"Will I have a lady's maid to tend to my needs?" I say.

"Would you prefer Anna Bates or that nasty one who made Lady Grantham slip after her bath?" Jeremy asks.

I'm relieved to hear he is up on his Downton Abbey characters.

"Anna Bates would be fine, thank you."

Chapter 21

"Never trust today's news."

*N**an never trusted the daily newspapers or TV nightly news. "Wait until tomorrow, or better yet, next week." She always felt that up-to-the-minute news was untrustworthy, out of context, too hot-off-the-presses. She liked magazine news, news where the editors had time to ponder the situation and report with a cool head. Her disdain of daily newspapers – not to mention 24-hour news channels – came from our stack of historic newspapers. People were always looking for the ones with two inch tall headlines when something momentous happened, like "Kennedy Slain" or the ones with erroneous headlines, printed before all the facts had been reported, like "Dewey Defeats Truman." We typically didn't have these famous ones, but we had a few old issues of our regional newspaper that were popular with sports fans, in a town where championships were so few and far between that historic newspapers were sometimes the best news there was.*

This afternoon, Spike and I have some historic news of our own to investigate. Spike and I snuggle together on Vittsjö with a soft fleece blanket and a hot cup of herbal tea to offset the caffeine shakes and calm the generalized anxiety a girl from New Jersey can get when she finds out her long-lost father isn't, as she has assumed, some sad soul her mother met at a bar for has-been actors, but rather the Earl of Heathwood, who is supposed to be addressed as – get this – *My Lord.*

The minute my laptop boots up, I google "Do illegitimate daughters of Earls have to address their fathers as My Lord?"

No results.

Spike starts bathing himself just rigorously enough to make my mug of tea begin to shake.

"Are illegitimate daughters of Earls considered nobility?"

No results.

"Do illegitimate daughters of Earls who were raised in America get British citizenship?"

No results.

"Are illegitimate daughters of Earls, who know they shouldn't be so greedy as to be asking this question, eligible for inheritance?"

No results. Come on, Google, help a girl out! I can't be the only illegitimate daughter of an Earl who has asked these questions.

Instead of just worrying about me, me, me, I decide to focus on learning more about my new family. And what I find is, well, *interesting*, to say the least.

My oldest half-sibling is my older half-brother, who is also illegitimate. Rob Bradley is in the hospitality industry, which after more strategic searching I find to mean that he bartends in a pub. On closer inspection, it is a pub outside of London which has been fined for numerous sanitation violations and once shuttered briefly for illicit drug activities. Drug dealing charges were brought against whom? The bartender by the name of Rob Bradley, of course. He is rumored by two different women to have fathered their children. He has made the news two other times, upon entering and exiting rehab. My heart hurts for this guy. I want something to go right for him, but it sounds like he's a walking disaster.

My other half-sibs are younger than I am. From what I can find, Alexandria Britton is pretty awesome. She's a mosaic artist by trade. But her mosaics aren't the frilly flowery kind. They all make a bold statement, with words hidden amongst the colorful melee. She is shaved completely bald, tattooed from head to toe, and angry as hell. Angry at the government. Angry at the Royal Family. Angry at capitalism. Angry at socialism. She was most recently spotted on hunger strike in New Zealand to save the kakapo, a type of endangered parrot. I impulsively make an anonymous donation to the Save the Kakapo fund. If no one else benefits from me finding my new family, at least the kakapo might.

Isabella Britton, the middle legitimate child, is simply pretty. She's got classic features that the rest of the Brittons – and I guess I'm including myself in that clan – don't seem to have been blessed with. She was a child model for a line of clothing and has dabbled in acting, including in two of the Earl's shows. She is engaged to a football player.

I realize I will need to come to terms with soccer being called football. I practice saying *football* while thinking *soccer* in my head and wonder how I will say this in front of my American friends without sounding like a complete poseur.

I study the pictures of Isabella closely. Apparently she is the one who sicced Jeremy and Ian on me in search of the necklace. Would she go so far as to order that they burgle my apartment? Did they actually find a way to open my safe and steal it? Apparently not, if they claim not to have found the necklace.

Isabella's Twitter account is getting more and more followers the more accolades her fiancé achieves on the football field and the more outrageously clad she is. As I lurk like a stalker through her past posts, it appears at one point as though she attained some bodily enhancements, at which point her followers quadrupled. In fact I start to wonder how I haven't heard of this person, as famous as she appears to be, at least in England.

The tabloids love her, too. In the world of tabloids, it is next to impossible to tell fact from fiction. She is alternately a drug-and-sex-addicted vixen manipulating her fiancé by promising access to the royal family or she is a philanthropy-minded volunteer for homeless shelters where she donates the haute cuisine leftovers from her star-studded gala events.

And last there's Jack Britton. My youngest half-sibling. He's a tech head. He even looks like one. He made the Forbes 30 under 30 list four years ago, heading up a start-up company that developed wearable technologies. But two years later, he was indicted for embezzling his venture capital funds and the company went under. He was acquitted last year, and then he founded a new company called, I kid you not, Mature Industries. Mature Industries' moonshot goal is to create the most humanlike sexbot on the market. And their investors are ponying up millions of dollars.

Seconds after I discover this, the ads popping up on my laptop switch from the snow boots I had been browsing on Zappos to the seediest looking dating sites and a host of confusing-looking sex toys that I would need a user's manual to understand. I erase my history and delete my cookies, but it is too late. Google sees me as a lonely sex fiend who wants to have sex with a robot. Good grief.

And my dad, aka *My Lord*? He's still directing movies and television shows. He seems to have never achieved beyond the small features and the B-list actors, but his filmography is a mile long. None of the shows are available on Netflix, but I do find a few scenes on YouTube. And they're not half bad. It's enough to know I want to see more.

I call Jeremy. "I've been on Google all afternoon. What's the deal with my family members?"

"How do you mean, exactly?" Jeremy asks, sounding concerned.

"Well, they're all kind of, I don't know..." I say.

"Screw-ups?" he suggests.

"Your words, not mine."

"Life in the spotlight isn't easy for most people. Look at the entire Royal Family. It's one scandal after another. The tabloids have made a whole publishing industry on airing their dirty laundry. It wouldn't be the Royal Family if it weren't scintillating," Jeremy chuckles.

"You're not making a very convincing case for my big reunion with the Earl," I say.

"No I suppose not. But the Earl is thrilled that we've found you. Do consider it, Grace."

"I have a question for you, Jeremy," I say.

"Ask away, my dear. Honesty suits me better than posing as a bumbling fool shopping for his wife in a junk sho —"

"Watch it!" I warn.

"Antique shop, pardon me," he corrects.

"That's better."

"And your question?" he asks.

"What was so special about the necklace that the

Earl's daughter Isabella sent you the whole way over the pond to find it? Why didn't you just call me?"

"It's a delicate situation. We didn't want to alert you to the value of the sapphire without knowing that we could trust you to sell it back to us, and not get into a bidding war with someone else."

"Let's say I had had the necklace in the store. Would you have paid me a fair price, if I had mistakenly had it displayed with the fakes?"

"I would hope we would have, yes."

"Honesty, Jeremy, honesty!"

"Okay, probably not," he confesses.

"Where do you think the necklace is?"

"No clue. Our best guess is that your mum gave it or sold it to someone. We've combed auction records, contacted high-end jewelers, asked all of our contacts. This is the kind of thing that would be talked about in the jewelry industry, given the size of the sapphire, but we haven't heard a thing."

"What did it look like?" I ask, feigning ignorance the best I can.

Jeremy proceeds to describe the necklace that up until my date night with Benjamin, had been sitting safely in my safe.

"The Earl had it specially designed for your mum, you know. It had been a brooch, but brooches were out of fashion in the U.S., and he had the royal Jeweler do it. Crown Jeweler Garrard. The jeweler – a nice gentleman with a stutter – met with him to talk design. The same jeweler who worked for the Queen, mind you. He spared no expense for your mother."

∞ ∞ ∞

I still don't know what to make of Jeremy, but he's growing on me, and I think he's being honest with me at last. And when I hang up the phone, I feel a weight lifting that I hadn't realized I'd been carrying around. I no longer think that Benjamin is lying to me. I really do believe that his father is the jeweler who accidentally swapped out Princess Diana's sapphire. And maybe I even believe that he actually likes me. Could it be that he's been telling the truth all along?

Which, holy shit, means that (a) I had and lost Princess Diana's sapphire, god rest her ever-stylish soul, in my bathroom mini-safe behind a stack of maxi-pads and (b) I have a really hot boyfriend. I'm not sure which of these is more incredible. But I know the second one makes me giddy.

I scoop up Spike and begin dancing around the apartment with him. When it comes to music, I'm not quite so vintage as to listen to disco. Love the shows, love the styles, but I can't quite take the music. I call up Alexa and she dials up some classic Madonna for me. Spike and I get into the groove, and it's only when I'm gyrating around the Dryzøk coffee table that I realize I have put Spike to sleep. He looks like such a sweet puff ball that I put him on my bed and lie down to snuggle.

I decide I finally need to come clean with Benjamin about the fact that I had the necklace and the mystery of its whereabouts now. I don't know how he will feel about me. Will he forgive me for lying? Like, lying repeatedly for the whole time I've known him? Surely with the value of the necklace, he will understand why I had to be extra careful, right? I said, right?

Deep breath, pick up the phone, and dial him. It rings three times, and then:

"Grace?" says a woman's voice.

"Who is this?" I say, trying not to panic.

"It's me, Fee, silly goose!" Felicity says in her usual upbeat voice. I must have dialed her by accident.

But no.

I didn't.

The weight that had lifted from my shoulders comes crashing back down in one heavy thud.

"Fee? What are you doing answering—"

"Gracie?" Now it's Benjamin's voice. "Gracie, baby, listen, it's not what it seems," he pleads. "We were j- j- just—"

I hang up.

Humiliation. Hurt. Jealousy. Madonna is now singing Crazy for You, and I curse out Alexa until the music stops.

Chapter 22

"If necessity is the mother of invention,
heartbreak is the mother of re-invention."

Nan counseled more than a few people when it came to heartbreak. The members of her Sisterhood could be shoulders to cry on more often than not. And I know she was always there for me through my puppy loves and high school crushes. But Nan herself seemed impervious to heartbreak. The few times I ever knew her to go on dates, she kept her wits about her and never got too attached to anyone. She said she'd learned her lesson with her first husband, my grandfather, and had come too far reinventing herself after that divorce to get subsumed by someone else's vision of who she should be. I wish I could be that steely.

"I knew Benjamin was too good to be true, but did it have to be my BFF?" I ask Geena the next morning. My eyes are puffy from crying myself to sleep using Spike as my pillow, triggering a mild allergic reaction that makes me look like I have pinkeye.

"That's rotten to the core," Geena agrees. I always got the sense she thought Felicity was too flaky for me. "But in my book, it's you who were too good to be true for Benjamin. He's the one who should be crying today, not you."

Benjamin has sent me no fewer than 25 texts since

last night, and I keep deleting them. Two more ping in, and I do the ultimate. I block his number.

"Was I only a fling to him?" I ask, my voice cracking as another round of tears wells up.

"Men don't know what they want, Grace. You know that. If I had to guess, he did believe in all those smooth words while he was saying them. What man in his right mind wouldn't fall for you? But they're weak too. Most guys can't turn down a woman like Felicity throwing herself at them."

"You'd think they'd have the decency to at least try to hide it," I say.

"Did he call you or anything?" Geena asks.

"He's been texting and calling all night and all morning. But there's nothing he can say to make it right."

"What's the breakup formula you once told me about? The number of months you dated, divided by 2 is the number of weeks you need to get over him?"

"Something like that, but we hadn't even dated for a month. So yes, part of me knows I'm being ridiculous!"

"Well, you're gonna feel what you're gonna feel. I say let me run the store today. You take the day off, do all the angry things you need to do, and start the healing process. Then after that, don't give him the power to make you feel this way. All right honey?"

Geena leaves to pick up a few things from home, telling me she'll be back in a half hour.

And just when I think the day can't get worse, it does just that. I look up as the doorbells jingle. Instead of the usual elderly customer, two very large police officers are standing together, putting their sunglasses in their breast pockets simultaneously. If Ben were here, he would know it. These guys look straight out of CHiPs.

For the love of God, why are the police here?

"Ma'am?" says the taller of the two officers, the one who looks like Ponch.

Immediately I start to cry.

"Is everything all right?" he asks.

"Yes," I say through my tears, "It's just that I've had a stressful morning, and the last time an officer talked to me, he called me Miss, not Ma'am, and I'm only thirty-one years old!"

He raises his eyebrow at the one who looks like the blond guy from CHiPs whose name no one ever remembered. "My apologies, Miss. May we ask you a few questions?"

Ponch steps in and begins the questioning.

"We are investigating a spate of burglaries in the area. I see your store has an alarm system. Was the alarm tripped at any time within the past two weeks?"

"No, but –"

"Is anything missing from your store's inventory?"

"No, but –"

"Any jewelry missing from the store?

"No, but –"

"Were there any signs of attempted entry?"

"No, but –"

Jesus H. Christ, these cops don't let you talk!

"Is there anything else unusual to report?"

"Yes!" I say. I wait for him to interrupt me again, but he's actually letting me talk.

"I have reason to believe," I say in my most official sounding voice, "that a piece of fine jewelry may have been stolen from a mini-safe in my apartment above the store, almost two weeks ago."

Ponch and the other guy look at each other, talking

with their eyes, and not sharing their secret conversation with me. Ponch flips open his notepad, ready to jot down an important finding.

"And the perpetrator let my pet rabbit escape!" I say, suddenly feeling the full violation of knowing that someone was in my apartment.

The officers roll their eyes at each other. That secret language was not hard to interpret.

"No, honestly, sorry, officers. I am missing a valuable necklace, but I cannot imagine how it was taken, given that I had it locked in a safe."

"And why didn't you report this to the police?"

Why hadn't I called the police? That's a very good question. Was I trying to protect someone?

"Long story," I say.

"Try us," Ponch replies.

"It all began before I was born," I begin.

"Not that long, please ma'am!" Ponch says.

"I said, I'm only thirty-one years old! It's not *that* long! And it's Miss, please!"

"Okay, let's begin again, Miss."

"I'll fast forward to when my mother died, four months ago. I was the executor of her estate, but I only got around to emptying her safe deposit box last month at the Wells Fargo, with the creepy looking teller who stares at women's chests and smells like moth balls. I got rid of most of the items, which were mostly paperwork, but there was one necklace that appeared to be valuable. So my ex-best-friend and I had a stupid dress-up party where I wore the necklace along with a low-cut vintage dress that was too tight. We got drunk off her cheap vodka, and then stupidly chose that night to program my mini-safe and store the necklace.

"Then two weeks ago, I was on a first date with a really attractive guy, and trust me, that doesn't happen to me often. When we came home to my place, the rabbit was missing and I felt someone had been in the apartment. Before we could really investigate, my date started violently vomiting, due to his shellfish allergy and having kissed me in the parking lot after I ate a shrimp tempura roll. It wasn't until yesterday that I carefully checked the safe, only to find the necklace gone. Gone straight out of a locked safe! To top it off, now the attractive guy is boffing my former best friend, and I have half a mind to see if they stole my necklace and plan to sell it off and elope together!"

The police stand in stunned silence. I can imagine they've dealt with plenty of crazies in their line of work. But something in their look tells me that I am the craziest of all.

Ponch nods at the other officer who says, "Er, Miss, if I understand your story correctly, and if I may remove some of the more colorful details, you retrieved a necklace from a safe deposit box last month from Wells Fargo, stored it in a mini-safe in your apartment, only to have it stolen two weeks ago?"

"Yes, that would be the Cliff Notes version," I say sheepishly.

"That squares with what our suspect is saying," Ponch says.

"What suspect?"

"The bank clerk from Wells Fargo."

"The bank clerk?"

"Yeah, the guy who smells like moth balls," Ponch clarifies.

I'm starting to feel sorry for Ponch's partner. He

doesn't get to say anything, just like in CHiPs. He's the wallflower compared with this Ponch guy. And while my mind is thinking about CHiPs instead of the real police in front of me, the name of Ponch's partner miraculously comes to me. He was Jon Baker. Jon Baker! Now come on. Couldn't the scriptwriters have done better than that?

"Wait a minute!" I say, coming out of my critique of the CHiPs writers and back to reality. "Are you saying the bank clerk stole my necklace?"

"It's an allegation. That's all it is, Miss. No arrest has yet been made," Ponch says.

"But isn't he, like, mere days away from the morgue?" I ask.

"Apparently not. His retirement funds went south in the last financial crisis, so he's still working at the bank when he'd hoped to be living in Florida now with an umbrella in his Metamucil cocktail. So he developed a side hustle. Swindling grieving people out of the contents of their loved ones' safety deposit boxes," Ponch explains.

"Hold on one second," I interrupt. "Can you please let the other guy talk? I suffer from an inferiority complex of my own, and it pains me to see your partner being sidelined."

More eye rolls.

"Okay," says the quiet one, hesitantly. "Here's his method. When the customers come to collect the items, they have to provide ID. This gives him access to their home addresses, which he records in a journal that he has shown to us under questioning. He's in league with a petty burglar expert lock picker who's not afraid to slip into someone's house and track down the valuables.

"We collared them both after our inside guy at the pawn shop flagged your necklace as suspicious. He'd never seen a jewel so large. He lets a lot of stuff slip under the radar, but this one he knew stolen."

"So wait a second," I say. "The burglar picked my lock, walked right into my apartment, and found the necklace, despite it being hidden behind my sanitary napkins and locked in a safe?"

Ponch and his partner groan.

"Your sanitary napkins?"

"Yes, the mini-safe was behind the maxi-pads."

"Not the maxi-pads! That's where any burglar worth his salt looks first."

"You're shitting me."

"God's honest truth," Ponch says.

"Dammit!" I say. "But how did he open the safe? It was supposed to be programmed to my fingerprint!"

"He tells us it was never locked. The display said, 'lift and rest finger to save touch ID,'" the quiet officer explains.

"You mean I never finished programming it? That damn cheap vodka!" I say.

"Yes, I think that's the case, Ma'am, er, Miss," Ponch says.

"Oh just call me Ma'am. I give up!" I say. "If a hundred-year old bank clerk, a petty burglar, and a biometric mini-safe can outsmart me, you can call me anything you want!"

"But the good news is, the bank clerk and the burglar have fully confessed, and with your testimony, we are ready to book them on charges. We've got the necklace. Which is more than we can say for most of their victims. All you need to do is come to the station to claim it."

Chapter 23

"Some days it's okay to play your B Side."

When I was growing up, I could be hard on myself, and Nan would tell me it's okay to play my Side B now and then. To most digital natives, this wouldn't mean much. But of course if you grew up alongside aging collections of vinyl and boxes and boxes of 45-speed records, you would understand.

As you might guess, the Side B of most albums wasn't as strong as Side A, but there were a few exceptions, as the philosophers of vinyl who frequented the store most Saturdays were quick to tell me. Some pointed out that Queen's We Will Rock You was the Side B of We are the Champions, and thank god the DJ's turned the record over, you know?

Like all kids, I had a few Side B moments growing up. Like the time I told Nan I was staying after school for debate club, when I was really making out with Jimmy Shanahan behind the 7-Eleven. He started kissing and groping me while I was still holding my cherry-cola Slurpee, which got pressed up against us, completely staining my shirt, which made the debate club lie hard to sustain.

I felt humiliated coming home to Nan with a wet t-shirt whose cherry-cola stain looked more like blood and mud. I could barely look Nan in the eye for the next week. I tried to repent by dusting the store, kissing up to customers, and organizing the basement shelves. But come to think of it, Nan *never said anything about the cherry cola incident at all. It was just me punishing myself. In retrospect, I think Nan was relieved that I was finally taking a few risks and testing my boundaries. She had started to worry that I was too sheltered — too much of a rule-follower to make it in the real world. And maybe she was right. Letting out the B side of our personalities is allowed to happen every now and then. It might even be good for us.*

The field trip to the police station takes my mind off my love life for the time being. Ponch and his partner offer me a ride to the station in their patrol car. Frankly I'm disappointed they aren't riding their highway patrol motorcycles. I wouldn't have minded hugging the quiet one as we sped down the highway into the sunset.

Reclaiming the necklace is surprisingly easy. I identify the necklace, sign a few papers, get dropped off back at my apartment, and say farewell to the CHiPs guys. At last I stow the necklace safely in the mini-safe—this time correctly in the sober light of day. I expect a feeling of relief or satisfaction to come with the necklace's safe return, but instead, the heartbreak comes rushing back.

So I start the first place any logical woman of the 21st century would start. I unfollow Felicity. But not before I see the photo she posted last night.

In the picture, Felicity has smashed her face up to Benjamin's cheek, and she herself looks completely smashed, and somehow sexy at the same time. She's wearing too much makeup and, is that body glitter? Christ! Do women still wear body glitter? She wrote, "Here's lookin at ya!" As if that makes any sense at all.

I study Benjamin's expression over and over again. I want to see some element of guilt or discomfort in his eyes, in his smile. But I don't. He looks perfectly pleased to be posing for a selfie with Fee, who's practically falling out of her chair and her shirt.

What's the second thing a broken-hearted woman does? Eat. Of course. Except I've got nothing in the fridge. I throw on a baseball cap and my comfiest fleece hoodie and make my way to the grocery store. At first, I try to be good. I grab a small bunch of bananas, and I even bag up a few apples, but when the uppity clerk says, "Hey, aren't you gonna weigh those apples?" I break down again. Out go the fruits, and in go the chocolates, the doughnuts, and the ice cream. Honestly, did I really think apples were going to cure my heartache?

You really can't beat Entenmann's rich frosted chocolate covered doughnuts when it comes to emotional eating. The creamy chocolatey frosting has just the right amount of magic-shell consistency to give each bite a satisfying snap that complements the cakey doughnut inside. They're so robotically reliable that they always taste exactly the same whether they're fresh out of the box or have been sitting in your cabinet for a week. But who's kidding who? They never last a week in my cabinet. Today is no different and they are the perfect companion for a mug of hot chocolate on the side, with a double packet of Swiss Miss.

Deep down in my heart, I know that eating half a box of doughnuts is not the way to get over my grief, but damn if it doesn't feel comforting. *Do I really need anything besides Entenmann's rich frosted donuts?*, I ask myself. I absentmindedly hand Spike a nibble, and he starts munching frantically, so I hand him some more. I've never seen him this ravenous, and honestly, he's probably never seen me this gluttonous.

We pass out together for an afternoon nap, which

feels glorious and luxurious until I wake up, and the whole breakup and deceit come back to my consciousness like a Mack truck in my brain.

It's time for step three in the playbook of broken hearts. The revenge hookup. I don't know what kind of illusion I am living under, but when I scroll through my contact list of past boyfriends, it doesn't give me a lot of options. Married, married, gay now, engaged, married with children, and down the list I go, until one name remains: Elvis. Yes, that's right, I dated a guy named Elvis O'Connor last year.

For all the times I wondered why a mother would name her clumsy daughter Grace, I could relate to Elvis O'Connor. He was teased mercilessly for the entire 40 years of his existence before he wandered into my store.

If nothing else, *Antique Junction & Etc.* is an accepting place. We don't judge. Honestly, we can't afford to. It's a place where a guy with the misfortune of being named Elvis will be welcomed with open arms. And not for nothing. We wouldn't be an antique shop without an homage to Elvis Presley in nearly every vendor's stall. When Elvis and I started dating, everyone was tickled that we had an Elvis to call our own.

Our personalities were a complete mismatch, but we boosted each other's confidence in ways that were good for both of us. He loved to be with a younger woman, or let's face it, *any* woman, and I loved that he doted on me, made me feel attractive, and took me to upscale restaurants that I couldn't afford. We eventually grew apart and parted as fond friends.

"Grace! To what do I owe the pleasure of your call?" He loved to put on a mock intellectual tone, but let's be real. He's just a kid from New Jersey like me.

"Why do exes normally call each other?"

"Needing a revenge shag? Who's the big jerk this time?"

I give him the less preposterous version of the story, leaving out the sapphires, royalties, the Downton Abbey bits, and the discovery of my father. I explain that it's gotta be tonight, because this is my one and only day of mourning for a two-week long love affair.

"I'd love to, you know I would, but I have a gig up in North Jersey tonight."

"A gig? I thought you were an accountant!"

"Remember when you said to be happy, I needed to 'own' my name? Well, I finally took that to heart."

"Yeah?"

"Yeah, I'm impersonating!"

"Impersonating, as in…"

"Elvis of course! I've finally put together a great backup band, and we're getting gigs every weekend. Who knew there was still a market?"

"Hang on, Elvis. You're a red-headed Irish guy covered in freckles from head to toe. How in the world are you impersonating Elvis Presley?"

"It's easy! Drag queen makeup! You can be anyone you want to be with drag queen makeup. And let me tell you, there is a whole world of postmenopausal women out there who love me!"

"Is that right?"

"Yes, it's amazing. The only biological clock they're worried about is the final countdown, and they're living large until then! I won't be lonely tonight!"

"Thanks a lot!" I say miserably.

"Oh geez, sorry Grace. Can I take a raincheck for a weeknight?"

Suddenly a night of Elvis music sounds like the antidote to my blues.

"Hey, Elvis?"

"Yeah?" His voice sounds kind.

"Can I come up and see your show? I promise I won't get in the way of any of your sex-crazed divorcees!"

∞ ∞ ∞

I meet Geena in the store. She tells me she sold an uncirculated coin set to a customer whose teenage son is interested in old coins. The boy has been fixated on coin dates since he was a young child, and now that he has a job at the supermarket, he's spending some of his earnings on coins.

"A teenaged numismatist!" Geena says. "I haven't met a young coin collector since I was young myself."

"Today's kids probably won't even know what cash is!" I say.

"Call me old-fashioned, but I like the feel of cash in my wallet. I like the designs on the bills and the coins. I like it that each country has its own system. It'll be a shame when all of that is gone," Geena says.

"Speaking of cash, we'll need some tonight. You and I are going out!"

Geena is nothing if not spontaneous, and she agrees to go to Elvis's show tonight. She always liked Elvis back when we were dating, and if an Elvis Presley impersonator two hours away in North Jersey isn't her favorite way to spend an evening out, she doesn't say so.

∞ ∞ ∞

The club has a Jersey feeling that is hard to describe. It's a combination of self-consciousness and faux glamour born of our constant inferiority complex living in the shadow of New York.

Older couples are sitting at tables near the back, some appearing to be lifelong partners and others taking part in the elderly dating scene, which is, sadly, more robust than my own.

Crowded near the front are the postmenopausal hotties that Elvis was telling me about. There's enough makeup in this room to fill a cosmetic store. And I don't even want to imagine the amount of money these women have spent on gravity-defying tactics. And the results are impressive. But who am I to judge? I'm quite certain a push-up bra will be in my not-too-distant future as well. I wonder which woman will catch Elvis's eye tonight.

Within moments, the lights dim, and the floor starts to rumble with the slow-build to the Space Odyssey intro music. I can see the outline of his band as the curtains part, and I honestly start to feel excited, like maybe, just maybe, the real Elvis Presley is going to come out on stage. Sure enough, as they break into CC Rider, a human being struts onto stage who looks like a wax museum sculpture of Elvis come to life. Elvis wasn't kidding about the drag queen makeup. I can't see a single part of his face that looks like the ginger-headed Elvis I know. I worry that the makeup might crack when he starts singing, but he appears to have it under control.

I look at Geena and I can tell she's thinking the same

thing I am. Elvis has completely transformed himself from the shy, awkward forty-year-old virgin who stepped into the store two years ago into the most convincing, pelvis-thrusting rendition of the King of Rock and Roll I have ever seen.

"Did you teach him the pelvis thing?" Geena asks.

"Ew, no! Do women really find that sexy? I love stage theatrics as much as the next person, but is that actually supposed to be attractive?"

But Geena doesn't answer. By this time, she has lifted her hands up in the air, dancing with the crowd. Elvis's voice bellows out through the room, with the colorful timbre of Presley's baritone melodies.

I am still observing the show with my usual dose of skepticism and irony, when I realize that Geena is totally immersed. And she looks many worlds happier than I feel. I want to be where she is. And so little by little, I let myself go. Before I realize what is happening, the drumbeats, the lights, and the sounds transport me to *Aloha from Hawaii Via Satellite*, where we are singing along with Blue Suede Shoes and applauding like star-struck teenagers.

I am one with the swooning women in the front, and I am convinced they are my best friends, through the sisterhood of Elvismania. The evening reaches a climax and I find myself shouting "We can't go on together, with suspicious minds (suspicious minds)!" sharing a collective anger toward all the many men who have hurt us, and a collective hope that the next one is as much of a hunk of burning love as Elvis the King.

Geena looks over with an expression of concern, and pulls me out of the club as Elvis is still riffing on a bigga bigga bigga hunka love.

"We end on a high note, baby," she says as we zip up our coats and head for the parking lot. I can hear the slow mournful strains of Can't Help Falling in Love, but we're not staying for that one.

We are both cracking up when we get in the car.

"Thanks for coming, Geena, I really needed that!"

"That may go down in history as the world's strangest revenge hookup, but I'm glad it brought you out of your funk," Geena says, still laughing.

"You know what I realized, about halfway through Hound Dog?"

"What, babe?"

"First, I have no idea what the lyrics in that song are supposed to mean,"

"Yea, me neither."

"And second, I'm not going to be crying all the time. Something big is happening in my life, and I'm gonna grab it."

I proceed to tell Geena the whole story of who that man in the picture is. I'm the daughter of an Earl who wants to meet me, and I have four step-siblings who, while all in various degrees of dysfunction, are still blood-relatives of mine. I've got bigger fish to fry than worrying about a cheating not-quite-boyfriend and a turncoat BFF.

Geena backs me up. Like she always has. I take her up on her offer to run the store and I call Jeremy the minute I get home.

"Blimey you Americans stay out late!" he says. But he is thrilled that I am coming to England.

I hang up quickly. I've got bags to pack. Which brings on my first panic attack. What should I wear when I meet my family?

Chapter 24

"Fashion is all an illusion."

I have had a love-hate relationship with fashion my entire life. Ask any self-identified curvy woman, and she will back me up. Nan, who shared my mother's lithe figure and not my own, would remind me it's all an illusion. And she's right, if you think about it. Fashions come and go like the wind. If I thought I looked good in low-rise jeans and dollar-store flip flops in early 2000, why do I suddenly look bad in that now? And if Mom jeans are coming back in style, does that mean they were never as dreadful as we once thought?

And can we talk about fashion shows? I don't understand how the outlandish costumes at a fashion show ever translate to what I'm buying at the H & M at the mall. Get serious, no one is going to wear a halter top made out of upcycled soda cans or butterfly wing shoulder pads or a Medusa crown made of dryer vent tubing. How can this be called fashion?

Not to mention, has anyone ever taken a moment to say to the fashion industry: What is up with women's sizes? If you are like any woman north of 20 years old who likes a good bowl of Ben and Jerry's, you will find that as you get older and your girth increases, the size of your clothing magically decreases. It turns out designers of women's clothing have been making the clothes larger to accommodate the growing waistlines in America, yet labeling the clothing with smaller sizes to make us feel better about ourselves. While this sounds like corporate empathy at its best, you eventually begin to wonder how long this deception can be sustained. After all, what are the skinny girls wearing? Negative sizes?

I am proud to say I now wear a size 12 in today's designer clothing, but honestly if I ever try on any of the vintage dresses in the store, chalk me up as a size 16. It's a travesty. But that doesn't mean those vintage ladies couldn't rock an outfit or two. I impulsively grab a few of the flashier 16's and hope to god they fit, because my flight is in two hours.

Next for my second panic attack. Where would you pack a priceless sapphire necklace that rightly belongs to the royal family of England? Carry-on luggage? In the zipper compartment of my wheelie suitcase? In a fanny pack?

I come up with what I hope is a brilliant idea. I put it in a small beat-up jewelry case that I've had for over ten years, and add five other costume necklaces of similar style, each wrapped in a plastic bag so they don't get tangled, and I throw in my makeup containers and other cosmetics so that the bag is packed full. I'm hoping this will camouflage this particular necklace from any prying TSA agents. I wear a costume necklace with a big fake ruby in the middle. It's something that would never be my style, but I'm ready to convince security that big splashy necklaces are the kind of jewelry I wear every day.

I get Spike ready for his babysitter. Bedding, lettuce, instructions, and my leftover brownies and doughnuts. I hope I return in time to take him to the vet for his teeth filing. He's getting a little long in the bunny tooth.

Geena's allergic to Spike, but Carla loves animals and has agreed to watch him for me. As for Carla and Ian, well, let's just say Carla was a stronger woman than Ian was looking for, and the love affair never made it out of the coffee shop. He had insisted on taking her out for dinner before taking her to bed, and she simply didn't have the patience for him.

I am relieved to find my passport is still valid, and only by a year. I stare at my passport photo, taken nine years ago, back when I lived in New York, before an ill-advised trip to Prague with the boyfriend du jour. I had once again rushed into a relationship, and by the time we had applied for our passports, gotten our photos taken, and waited for the processing, he had found another girl-friend who apparently preferred Paris.

But not all was lost. I was visiting Nan the weekend he dumped me, and on a whim, I asked the young woman I'd met once or twice who worked up the street from Nan's store and did Nan's jewelry repairs.

"Prague? Why do you want to go to Prague anyway? Let's go to Cancun!" Felicity said.

And before you know it, we had our bags packed with string bikinis, romance novels, and sundresses. I jumped into a friendship with Fee as fast as I had jumped into bed with that boyfriend, whose name I can't even remember. But that's the thing with girlfriends. You can trust them in a way you can never quite trust a man in your life. At least that's what I thought --until now.

∞∞∞

British Airways is the best way to fly. And much to my surprise, I discovered I've been moved to first class. I am wrestling to stow my carry-on in the overhead when the man in front of me offers me a hand. His eyes are warm and his close cut beard frames his features.

"Lovely necklace," he says, his eyes drifting past my necklace. In a silent message of revenge to Benjamin, I am wearing the scoop neck sweater that made his eyes go wide on our first date. I've packed every eclectic vintage top along with all the form-fitting clothing that I've stored in the back of my closet, waiting for a skinnier day, waiting for a hot date, waiting for the courage to wear it in public. Well, that day is here.

Because this is the new me. I am not hiding behind frumpy tunics anymore. I am the daughter of the Earl of Heathwood. I've got to live up to expectations of the royal family after all. And that means one thing and one thing only: It's time to dial up the scintillating.

With thinly veiled intentions, I convince the old woman sitting next to the window in the bearded man's row that she would prefer my aisle seat a row back. This requires me to brush up against the man as I'm squeezing past him to get to the window seat. I can feel the temperature rising already.

How much can really take place in an airplane seat on a five-hour flight?

A lot, as it turns out.

Ryan, his name is, is going to Germany to see a soccer match, excuse me, *football* match, which seems extravagant to me, but extravagance may just be part of my new lifestyle. He is just getting over a breakup too, like of an actual girlfriend of nearly a year, and flirting with me is just what the doctor ordered. He starts out slow and awkward, but by the time we are on our third gin and tonic, he is full of every sexual innuendo ever imagined, and were it not for the seatbelts, and the fact that the first class flight attendants are so ruthlessly attentive, some serious snogging could be occurring.

What's remarkable is that I don't do anything clumsy for the entire five hours. No spilled drinks, no faux pas. This guy Ryan is the guru of building my confidence.

"It's funny, we only met a few hours ago, and I feel like I know you already," he says.

"Nah-uh, no, nope, that's a bad one, Ryan. All guys say that. It's one step away from the 'don't I know you from somewhere' pickup line. Try another one," I suggest.

"Okay, well, it's just that I feel like I can be myself when I talk to you," he tries.

"Overused. Heard it before. You need some help if you're going to be dating again, Ryan. It's not easy out there. Give it one more try," I say.

"What about, your sweater is making me horny as hell?" he says.

"Points for honesty. Should we order another one?" I ask.

He's a total sweetheart and after several hours side by side with me has completely aced the art of flirting, but I think we are both relieved in a way when the flight is over. When we come into the light of the terminal, and it's six in the morning British time, neither one of us looks so good and the jetlag hits like a ton of bricks. He heads off for his connecting flight, while I make my way to baggage claim, both of us feeling just a little more confident in ourselves.

Chapter 25

"Before spouting off your opinion, look at the situation in reverse."

Nan said it was always better to look in the mirror before jumping to conclusions. Any opinion, criticism, or judgment could benefit from a little self-reflection first. She called this looking at it in reverse. She was fascinated with the concept of mirror images and could even write backwards as neatly as she could write forwards. I liked to hold up her secret messages to a mirror to decipher little notes that she would stick in my lunch box.

When I was young, I was mesmerized by the old-fashioned letterpress typeset trays and the little backwards letters in them. One of our vendors always seemed to have one or two examples of these sets, and they usually sold fairly quickly to collectors. I loved the small compartments, often of differing sizes, where in the old days, a printer would organize the different letters of the alphabet. Each letter stamp was molded in reverse, so that when the ink was rolled on it, and then pressed upon the page, the letters would print in the correct direction. Considering I was terrible at spelling in my school days, I couldn't imagine how hard it was to manually typeset every single letter of a daily newspaper with no errors. This still amazes me today.

But where I lack in spelling, I am great at reading mirror images thanks to Nan and those cool typesetting stamps.

I arrive at customs and have visions of them searching my bag and discovering Princess Diana's missing sapphire and hauling me off to the Tower of London. But the customs agent seems as impressed by my sweater as Ryan was, and waves me along after a quick ogle.

I am expecting a dignified butler to be holding up a sign with my name, and to drive me off in a limousine to a castle, where my father will be wearing an ascot and drinking aged single malt scotch.

But all I see is a crowd of people finding their way to their taxis, Ubers, and loved ones. I'm about to send Jeremy a text asking where the hell I'm supposed to go, when the crowd parts like the dance scene in *West Side Story*, and I am staring across the lobby at an older more masculine vision of myself. It's like Heathrow has set up a gender-bending mirror, and I'm looking right at it.

He's not wearing an ascot. He's wearing black jeans, an oxford, and a sports coat. His hair is salt-and-peppered and wavy. And it's just long enough to look tussled, but not so long that he's trying to relive his youth. I have to admit, for an old guy, my father looks pretty hip.

"Grace?" he says, as he walks toward me.

I am numb. In addition to the way you would feel if you've met your father after 31 years of thinking you would never find him, my immediate issue is that I don't know what I'm supposed to call him. He seems to read my mind.

"You can call me Alex, if you'd like," he says.

I'm still mute. It hasn't computed in my head that my father would speak with a British accent. But of course, he does.

"Should we shake hands?" I say, and immediately cringe. Is that really the first thing I say to my father? Apparently, it is.

He laughs and shakes my hand using both of his.

"C'mon," he says, grabbing one of my bags. "We've got a lot to catch up on."

∞ ∞ ∞

As we roam the parking garage together, he stops in front of a blue VW Golf and opens the passenger door for me.

"You're wondering where the limousine is? The paparazzi? *The Daily Mail?* My footman?"

Man, this guy can read my mind.

"I'm disappointingly regular, if you haven't sorted that out already," he says.

"I'm not disappointed," I say, and while not a dazzling conversation starter, at least I'm talking, and I'm telling the truth. He has a warm and easy-going nature, not something that matches up with my stereotype of British nobility.

We finally break free of the traffic on the highway, excuse me, *motorway,* and start cruising along at a steady clip. It's easier to talk to him while we're both staring at the road.

"My family sold most of the Heathwood estate twenty years ago. It was just too expensive to maintain. It was the best decision they ever made. Apart from the occasional news-making tidbit from my children, we can keep a low profile and live normal lives now."

"Have you told anyone about me?" I ask.

"Quite!"

"Quite?"

"Quite right! My whole family knows and can't wait to meet you."

"They weren't angry with you?" I ask.

"Angry? They're thrilled! You see, the odd messing about outside your marriage is not so unacceptable here as it is in the States."

"It didn't sound like odd messing about in the love letters you sent my mom," I say.

"She saved them, did she?" he says, blushing a little.

"How long did you stay in contact with her?" I ask.

"On and off for many years. Right after my divorce, I may have scared her away for a few years. She thought I wanted more, and the truth is, I did want more. It was all I really wanted, actually, to be with her. But at the end of the day, I was only an on-again off-again interest for her."

"She was kind of a rolling stone in the love department," I say. "Lots of boyfriends, but no one ever stuck around long. I have to think she kind of wanted it that way."

"My guess is she was protecting you."

"By not ever even telling me who my father was? By having the revolving door of boyfriends? I loved my mom, don't get me wrong, but it wasn't what I would call a stable childhood."

"But look at you, love," he says.

"What about me?"

"You've turned out fantastic! Jeremy tells me you're an intelligent woman, running your own business, and a downright expert on all things antique, retro, and Americana. If I had to guess, and trust me, I've been doing a lot of soul-searching since Jeremy told me about you, I think she didn't want you being a part of all this," he says, gesturing up and down and around the car.

"All this?"

"Well, yes, I meant to say that with more of a flourish, but you can't really do flourish in a VW Golf. What I mean is, she didn't want you growing up as a British noble. She didn't want a tabloid story about you being born illegitimately to the Honorable H. Alexander George Britton. And they would have been on top of that back then. They would have painted me like a playboy and tracked down you and your mother. She saw what was going on with my son Robert and his mother and didn't want any part of that. For you or for herself. That's what I mean by protecting you."

I think about that for a while, and it makes some amount of sense.

"I raised three children at the estate, Alexandria, Isabella, and Jack. Growing up with that kind of opulence, the expectations, the public scrutiny. I'm not sure I did them the best service," he says forlornly.

"I can't exactly say I feel sorry for you. We were living hand to mouth on my mother's Macy's wages for so many years. Couldn't you have at least sent her a little cash now and then, even if it was just this fake Monopoly money," I say, studying the five-pound note he has crumpled up on the dash.

"I tried more than once. She was too proud to accept it. If I had known she was raising a child – our child or any child – I would have insisted."

"Were you the one who got her the acting gigs?"

"I'd like to think I helped, especially if that helped to bring money in the door, but I imagine she got them on her own talent. She was a better actress than she gave herself credit for," he says.

"I'm nervous about meeting your kids. You can't imagine what it feels like to grow up as an only child and suddenly find out you've got siblings," I say.

"They will love you. They're coming Saturday night. Until then, welcome to my estate!"

∞∞∞

Alex lives on a cobble-stoned hill in a modest stone house connected along a row of homes with chimney pots, leaded windows, and wood shingles. These are houses right out of a storybook. One thing for sure: I am not in New Jersey anymore.

His spare bedroom is set up for me, with towels, soaps, and a package of Hobnob biscuits, and I'm ready to collapse on the bed the minute I see it.

"Have a bath, I'll put on some tea. Whatever you do, don't fall asleep! You've got to push through the jetlag so you'll be fresh to meet my kids – I mean, my *other* kids – on Saturday."

Over the course of the day, Alex and I figure out how to move around each other, giving space where space is needed, and sharing bits of ourselves gradually when it feels right.

I finally lie down in bed as early as Alex deems reasonable to get me on the right time zone, and I feel a sense of gratitude. I'm grateful that I have this opportunity to meet my father. I'm grateful that my life is expanding out from my little shop in New Jersey across the big pond to a whole new world of relatives, histories, and narratives that are now part of my story.

I'm dying to share this with someone, most of all Felicity, and my heart sinks back into sadness as sleep overtakes me.

∞∞∞

I wake to a soft sunlight filtering through the curtains, when I realize it's not sunlight, but moonlight. It's 3am and I am wide awake. I hear my phone buzzing softly, and I accept the call without thinking.

"Gr- Grace?"

"Who's this?"

"It's Benjamin! I finally figured out you were b-blocking my number, so I'm dialing from a p-p-prepaid."

"Why are you stuttering? Are you drunk?"

"I've always had a stutter! It's the b-b-bane of my life!"

"But you didn't stutter before!"

"That was the magic of you, Grace. I didn't stutter when I was with you. It's c-come back with a v-vengeance since you've g-ghosted me."

"You're shitting me again!" I say, and then I hear a voice in the background.

"Where are you?" I demand.

"I'm with F-F-Felicity, but it's not w-w-what it---"

"How can it be anything other than what it seems, Benjamin?" I say in an angry whisper, because I don't want to wake up Alex two doors down.

"Just l-let me explain," he begins.

"Aw Benji," I hear Felicity's voice say in her usual drunken slur, getting louder in volume as she gets closer to the phone. "Just give it up."

I hang up. It's too much to hear them together like that. I know how Felicity is when she's drunk, and I am sure she's all over him at this exact moment while I am lying by myself in a twin-sized bed, all alone and wide awake.

I text Carla and Geena to make sure everything is okay back home, and I send them the selfie I took with Alex. Carla says Spike is being moody and won't come out of his corner, but is still the cutest furball anyone could ask for.

I pad over to my suitcase and unpack my clothes into the empty drawers Alex cleared for me. I check the necklace, and it's still tucked safely into the plastic bag in my jewelry case. Tomorrow is the day I'm going to return it to Alex. I've decided I like him. I trust him. And I think he will be thrilled to return it to his daughter Isabella. I've brought the love letters too. Those I think he will cherish even more.

But I'm still wide awake and still seething about Benjamin's call. Like always happens when I can't focus, I feel the need to rearrange. Alex has got all the furniture in the small bedroom lined up along the walls. The bed is right up against the window where a draft is coming in, so I pull it out so it sticks out into the bedroom. I move two small tables on either side of it and adjust the lamps so I can read in bed. This means the dresser and chair need to move on opposite sides. I manage to slide them across the floor quietly, and by the time I've finished, I'm ready to doze off again. I finally drift off to sleep, too tired to be angry anymore.

Chapter 26

"Go ahead and cry over spilt milk. No one should tell you what you can and can't cry over."

At one point in our store's history, we had no fewer than ten of those antique milk cans. You can picture them, right? The handles, the lid? It's the kind of jug that fits right in with a quaint country kitchen, perhaps with a pot of fake flowers on top.

I like to imagine the halcyon days when milk was delivered from the dairy farms in these 10-gallon cans, and women would meet the milk trucks with their containers to the get them filled up. But it only takes one coronavirus pandemic in your lifetime to get kind of skeeved by the idea. Imagine unpasteurized milk being poured into these unsterilized metal cans, sitting in the sun all day, as people lined up to have milk ladled out. And how did they keep it cold at home? Sometimes I'm not convinced the halcyon days were all that halcyon after all.

Alex putters around the kitchen and fiddles with the coffee maker. I can tell he never makes coffee, because the bag of ground coffee is brand new and he doesn't even know how to open it. I don't know whether to make myself at home in his kitchen. It's not like he's been my dad all my life and it's not like I know my way around his kitchen. But he looks hopelessly lost with the coffee grounds, so it's now or never. I stand up and reach out my hands.

"I know, I'm rubbish at this. Why can't they just put the coffee in a teabag? Does it take a genius to work that out?" he says, scratching his head.

"You stick with the lightly flavored tea water, I'll handle the real fuel," I say. I'm going to need a strong one to make up for the jetlag and the sleep I lost last night rearranging the bedroom to avoid thinking about my love life.

"I can't believe all my kids drink coffee. You, I'll give you a pass, growing up in the States. But my English-born kids? How can they desert a lonely old man like that when all I ask is to come over for tea now and then?"

"Has Starbucks overrun the UK too?" I ask.

"Starbucks and Costa Coffee. Seems every other storefront is people buying expensive coffee. Meanwhile the lowly teabag is relegated to a drink of old farts."

One thing Alex has decidedly mastered is his toaster. Two perfectly toasted slices of bread pop up just as we have poured our drinks, and we settle in the breakfast nook. He hands me a section of the newspaper, which I deeply appreciate, because it feels too early to be socializing about 31 years worth of life experiences.

The coffee finally starts doing its job, and I feel human again. I pad over to the bedroom in my British Airways fuzzy socks (who doesn't love an airline that gives out fuzzy socks?) and come back to the kitchen nook with my jewelry case.

"You are kidding me, Grace! You've had the necklace all along?" Alex asks, stunned when I pull out the baggie from my jewelry case.

"Yes, if you don't count when it was stolen from my

supposedly foolproof mini-safe, that apparently can be outsmarted by a hundred-year-old bank teller who smells like moth balls."

"So you knew it was valuable?" Alex asks.

"Since the day I opened my mom's safe deposit box last month, yes. I loved the way the gem shined up at me, even in the dim lighting of the bank vault room. My ex-best friend who's a jeweler confirmed it was the real deal."

"Ex-best friend?"

"Long story, but she's sleeping with my ex-boyfriend."

"Which one was ex first?"

"It was simultaneous," I explain.

"Ah, got it," Alex says with a sympathetic grimace.

"I had it for only a couple weeks and was still trying to figure out what to do with it, when your two nattering *goons* showed up in the store!" I say with a teasing voice.

"Jeremy and Ian?" Alex chuckles. "Yea, maybe I should have sprung for professionals. But they'd been checking in with your mum over the years, so they were already familiar with the store, and we thought the necklace might have ended up there."

"Ah, the two mysterious British gentlemen that my Nan noted. She kept track of every time they showed up in the store. Why have they been looking for the necklace for so long? Couldn't you just have asked her for it in one of your love letters?"

"I didn't want the necklace back from your mother."

"Then your goons were just, what, spying on my mom?" I say, feeling all of a sudden like I shouldn't have trusted Alex so quickly.

"It wasn't spying," Alex laughs. "They were casting agents, not just for my company but several other production companies. They're retired now. But they used to take an annual trip to the States, and if the roles were right, they'd sometimes meet with your mother. She'd listed the store as her address, so I think they ended up meeting your Nan too."

"Yet they never knew about me until just last week?"

"I can only guess you must have been at school. They honestly never knew."

I feel like a clod for never asking Jeremy and Ian what they did for a living, but it's starting to make more sense now.

"Jeremy is the one who convinced me to come meet you," I say, handing the necklace to Alex.

Alex smiles, but won't take the necklace from me as I try to hand it to him.

"Don't you see," he says, "Now that I know you exist, there's no one more fitting to have the necklace than you, Grace. I gave it to your mother with all of my heart, and now you've inherited it from her. I couldn't think of a better person to have it."

"But what about Isabella? Jeremy said she was the one who wanted you to retrieve it. Don't you want to keep it in the family?" I say.

He looks at me with one eyebrow raised.

"Oh, duh," I say, "I guess I *am* the family."

"Isabella has more jewelry than Tiffany & Co. I think she'll survive," he says dryly.

Next I give him the love letters and the one torn photograph that had led me to him. I've reaffixed the piece of the photo showing the necklace. It's not the world's best patch job, but it was all I had to work with.

Upon seeing the photo, his eyes start to tear up, and I'm worried that he might cry. Please, please, don't start crying. I try to send my plea to him via telepathy, through whatever DNA we share in common, and it seems to work. He quickly pulls himself together. I didn't fly the whole way to England to comfort a heartsick Earl. Not to be a selfish long-lost illegitimate daughter, but I want this trip to be about me, not him. Is that asking too much?

"What I loved most about your mother was her zest for life. It was a breath of fresh air, compared with the stodgy British ways back then. My marriage, well, it was right and proper for an Earl's son to be married to a woman from the aristocracy, wasn't it? But when I met your mother, my worldview shattered in a million pieces, and I saw the aristocracy for what it was. Did I have the courage to leave it? No, I felt I owed it to my family to keep up pretenses."

"Why'd you fall so hard for my mom anyway?"

"She was bright, optimistic, open-minded, and had this vision of the future where the arts were the great equalizing force, bringing everyone together. She was a delightful actress. I was ready to cast her about 20 seconds into her first audition. In retrospect, I should have cast her as the lead, but she just hadn't had the experience yet.

"I've followed her career of course. I always wondered why her career didn't blossom into much more," Alex says.

"I guess it couldn't have been easy raising me while trying to get parts. My Nan was always there to help, but still, she had a lot to juggle. I remember when she did get cast, she'd be gone for weeks at a time. I know she loved me, but I am sure some days she resented all the mom duties, you know?"

"And she probably resented that I wasn't a part of your life to pull my share of the work. I do wonder how things might have been different had I known about you, Grace," he said glumly. "She never married? Never settled down with anyone?"

"Nope, a revolving door, like I said. But I think the fact she saved your letters all those years means you really meant something to her, right?" I say, trying to make him feel better.

"I suppose giving her the necklace was a rather extravagant gift, but I was smitten. And she loved the sparkle and glitter of fine jewelry. She could hardly resist it. It felt like my own little rebellion, I have to admit, gifting her one of the jewels that was part of our family collection back then."

"How did you explain it away? Wouldn't it have been noticed as missing?"

"Oh it's quite terrible, really. I'm embarrassed to admit it, but I paid to have a cheap artificial sapphire made into a brooch for my then wife. She kept it in the divorce settlement, and I never found the courage to admit that it was a fake. I think she guarded it with her life and never actually wore it. It was only a few months back when she was showing her jewelry to our daughter Isabella that Isabella spotted it as a fake. I claimed no knowledge of it, given that I hadn't seen the piece since our divorce, but Isabella wasn't buying it, and wrenched the truth out of me, thus setting Jeremy and Ian on the case, who were all too happy for another visit to the U.S."

"Jesus, Alex, I'm not feeling all warm and fuzzy about you right about now. You're a two-timing thief of your own family's most precious heirlooms!" I say.

"I admit it doesn't sound good on paper," he says. "But if you had lived a minute with my ex-wife, you would understand.

"Basically from the day we got married, she was threatening divorce every time I so much as sneezed. Her family was made up of loads of barristers who would have taken me to the cleaners, so I would have lost the family heirlooms to her anyway, and I sure as hell didn't want the sapphire going to her when it matched your mother's eyes so beautifully."

"What happened when you finally did get divorced?" I ask.

"Exactly that. She pretty much took everything valuable that we had in our collection, but nothing quite as lovely as the sapphire in my opinion.

"That was the one and only thing that she and your mother shared in common. A love of fine jewelry. My ex loved it for the status. More than that, she loved having reasons to wear it, and signed us up for every charity ball within a 100-mile radius. Whereas your mother loved it for its beauty. Pure and simple. A sapphire that stunning belonged in the hands of your mother, and now you."

Shit, I think, things are not going as I had schemed it. If I'm honest, I was hoping to pawn off the problem of Princess Diana's precious sapphire to the Britton family and walk away with, I don't know, an aristocratic monthly allowance? A trust fund? A pied-à-terre in London? If I made some nice family connections, fine, but chiefly, I was hoping to wash my hands of this little sapphire problem and bring a little prosperity into my life.

But between the VW Golf and the run-down cottage, I'm not feeling a fountain of wealth, and the fact that he's giving the necklace right back to me is putting me in a bind. The necklace would fetch a good price, but I can't honestly *sell* a crown jewel, you know? And I can't exactly walk up to Buckingham Palace and ask if I could swap out the jewel from the dead Princess's famous necklace. I need somewhere quiet to think this through. So for now, we do the cleaning up and chit chat about the day ahead.

∞∞∞

Alex is gracious enough to allow me to have the bathroom first. It's a strange thing, glimpsing into the life of another person via their bathroom. The first thing I do is open the medicine cabinet. Hair dye, generic drug-store cologne, unidentifiable creams, a box of condoms. What am I doing snooping in his cabinet? All of this I would be just as happy not to have seen. None of these items seems befitting of an Earl, much less a man who seems to be my father. I quickly shut the cabinet and turn on the shower. The ancient British plumbing shudders and clangs and the water feels one degree warmer than ice for at least five full minutes.

It finally warms up, and I hear Alex shout, "Ten minutes tops before the hot water runs out!" With the weak trickle from the shower head, I'm wondering how I will even get my hair wet in ten minutes. I'm in full shampoo lather when the reality of Alex's warning sets in and the ice shards start raining down on me. I shiver my way through the rest of the shower, and step out onto the cold tiles, which feel warm in comparison to my arctic shower.

The charm of Alex's cottage is quickly giving way to my desire for the creature comforts of an anonymous hotel chain with powerful hot showers and no embarrassing personal effects in the cabinet.

Alex greets me with a fresh cup of tea and a blanket, so that I can recover while he's taking his shower. And as

I bundle up in the cozy blanket, and look across the small living room, I feel the steam of the teacup rising up under my chin. I am surprised to discover that the tea truly is comforting. There's no place I'd rather be at this moment than under this blanket cradling a cup of hot tea. I miss Spike and I'm still heartbroken, but the magical therapeutic benefit of this cup of tea at this exact moment is just what the doctor ordered.

When Alex emerges showered and shaved, he claps his hands, ready for our day's activities.

Which, it quickly becomes apparent, he has not planned out at all. He has no idea what to do with a 31 year old daughter he's known for 24 hours, and I myself don't have any clue what is even possible in this quaint English village that suddenly feels as remote as Siberia.

But my quiet time with the cup of tea has allowed me to think and come to an important conclusion. I need to escape the burden of the necklace. I need to tell all.

"My ex-boyfriend has also been searching for the necklace," I begin.

"Searching for the necklace? Now hold on a minute. Your ex-boyfriend isn't Ian, is it? That randy bastard!"

"Ew, no, give me some credit."

Alex laughs.

"Why would your boyfriend be searching for your mum's necklace?"

"Ex-boyfriend," I correct.

"Yes, why would your ex-boyfriend be searching for your mum's sapphire necklace?"

"Because I never told him I have it. So he's still looking for it."

"You mean he's been looking for it ever since the banker who smells like moth balls stole it from your bloody useless mini-safe?"

"No. My ex-boyfriend, before he was ever my boy-friend in the first place, showed up at my store searching for the necklace the same day Jeremy and Ian did."

"Okay, forgive me for being dense, but how in the world does he know it even exists?"

"His father made the necklace," I say.

Alex looks completely dumbfounded. And why wouldn't he?

"His father is the jeweler who made the necklace 31 years ago?" he asks.

I proceed to describe Benjamin, leaving out the sexy bits, along with the fact that Princess Diana's sapphire choker was in for repairs, followed by the royal jewel mix-up, and his father's years-long search for the sapphire, and his death bed wish to make things right.

"Princess Diana's famous sapphire? Bloody hell, you mean I gave your mother Princess bloody Diana's sap-phire? The Windsor's gem? How has no one noticed this before?"

"They're close to identical. The one in the Windsor family's necklace is a close enough match to the naked eye, but according to Benjamin, a jeweler can easily spot the difference by looking at it through a loupe."

"It's a good thing I could give a rat's arse about my rank, because my goose is cooked if this ever hits the news. I'll stir up more controversy than all my wayward children combined."

"But why, if it was never your fault? Wouldn't it hurt Benjamin's jewelry business more than your reputation?"

"Oh dear, is the media that much different from the media here? It's simply whatever will sell the papers. An Earl embezzling the late and beloved Princess Diana's precious sapphire is far more entertaining than a jeweler whom no one has heard of."

"I guess you're right. You can make a viral sensation out of just about anything these days."

"It's a fate I'd rather avoid if I could."

Alex places an urgent call to Crown Jeweler Garrard and by noon, he has heard back from Benjamin's father. He's not well enough to make the trip, so Alex agrees to meet him at his shop, with the sapphire necklace, Saturday afternoon.

"I've never heard relief as palpable as his. He thinks he can arrange with the Crown Jeweler to perform maintenance work on the late Princess's sapphire choker and make the switch then, hopefully with no one ever being the wiser," Alex said. "I think we've met a dying man's wish. Sad, really, but it will be good to set it right. No pun intended."

I feel so relieved that I've finally shared the truth with Alex, and doubly relieved that he took it in his hands to solve the problem.

Chapter 27

*"A handwritten letter is to a text message
like fine dining is to fast food."*

*N*an remembered fondly the days of sending letters to friends. She'd written scores of letters in her day. To her first steady boyfriend who was deployed overseas, to a friend whose husband's job moved them across the country, to a pen pal she was matched up with as far back as grade school. She'd even written postcards to her girlfriends in the Sisterhood when she so much as took a vacation down the shore without them.

Nan never appreciated the fine art of a good text. She would see me texting my friends, or occasionally a boyfriend, and just shake her head at the disposable, meaningless nature of our rapid-fire volleys. The first time a guy broke up with me by text, Nan was horrified. "Is that even legal?" she asked.

I think about the letters that my mother and Alex wrote to each other, and how their relationship – if that's what you would call it – grew through these letters, and how the letters are still meaningful to Alex now. Given her dismissal of so many men, it still stunned me that these letters were meaningful enough to my mother that she saved them for so many years.

That clearly is not the way my brief relationship with

Benjamin began or ended. It was all too lightning fast. It never had the chance to mature, yet I can't help feeling like he's making a mistake with Fee. Not that Fee isn't super fun to be around, but she just won't get him the way I did. His quirky sense of humor isn't any more her style than are last year's clothing trends.

I decide to accompany Alex on the trip to London the next day. Maybe it's not half bad to spend the day hanging out with my father. If I can't let a relationship unfold correctly with a boyfriend, at least maybe I can try to develop a functional relationship with the man who turns out to be my father. It still sounds strange to say "father," but I'm coming around to it.

I've never been to London. It's not that I haven't wanted to, but until now, the funds have never been there for much international travel, except my one-off trip to Cancun with Felicity. I expect it to feel like Manhattan, but it feels about as much like Manhattan as Cheerios taste like Fruit Loops.

Alex starts me out at Camden Market, which is a sea of people looking at an ocean full of tchotchkes, tourist t-shirts, hand-crafted items, street foods, eclectic clothing, jewelry, and other bric-a-brac. It's like *Antique Junction & Etc.* on methamphetamines.

He buys a cappuccino and a hot tea from a street stall and we find an empty curb to sit on along the canal. Behind us are tourists speaking every language imaginable, and I love the frenetic pace of movement all around me.

He burns his tongue on the first sip of tea, and goes to remove the lid, causing the hot liquid to spill out onto his blue jeans.

"Bloody hell, I'm so clumsy," he mumbles.

"Another genetic mystery solved," I laugh, handing

him a wet wipe. "I always carry these in my purse for just that reason. And a Tide stick too."

"So you haven't told me much about your life, love."

"You mean, what was my mother like? What was it like being her daughter?"

"No, Grace, I mean what are *you* like? Are you happy in your work? Are you doing the things you like in your life?"

I look at him sidelong. This is not the fairytale reunion I had once imagined between daughter and father, sitting on a dirty curb with all these tourists jostling around behind us and the cappuccino tasting like it was made from an instant mix, but I get the feeling he genuinely wants to get to know me. He's letting things slowly unfold in a way that's telling me he intends to keep me in his life for the long haul.

I tell him about growing up with my Nan and my mom and my failed attempt at making it on my own in New York. I haven't told many people about what hit me hardest in New York City. It wasn't only the job failures, the high rent, and the sheer and utter density of other human beings all living on one tiny island. No, it wasn't any of that. It was simply that I liked myself better whenever I came home to New Jersey. I felt at home and completely myself. No more pretending, no more competing, no more dating men who were more ambitious than amorous, no more networking frantically looking for the next best thing. I could wake up, do my job, and simply be myself.

I give him the lo-down on the community of people at the store who are my substitute family. And as I'm talking, I grow wistful for Geena, Jakob, and Carla, and fonder than I ever thought possible. I even think about George, the bartender at Puke's Tavern, with the mildly protective glances he sends my way whenever a guy is chatting me up.

I lighten up the mood by telling him about Ian's encounter with the voluptuous Carla at the coffee shop.

"Ian met a woman who's more sex-crazed than he is?"

"Sounds like it!" I laugh.

"What about you? Tell me more about what happened with the ex."

Something about being engulfed in the cacophony of a thriving tourist attraction makes me feel like it's a safe place to tell all. And I do.

"I felt like he knew me inside and out before we even said a word to each other," I say. "Not like I believe in love at first sight. I'm 31 years old after all. But it felt like something was really there."

"Well if you are a romantic, you can blame that on genetics, too," Alex adds.

And then I tell him about the heartbreak and the traitorous friend, and I can see him cringing for me, and possibly even getting angry for me. It is then I know he's in my corner. And I can't deny that feels pretty good. Maybe meeting my father 31 years later than most people do might not be all that bad.

"And you've heard nothing from either of them? Nada?" Alex says.

"Benjamin keeps trying to call me, but what is there to say? I can't bear knowing they're together. I'm better off going cold turkey from both of them."

"Maybe he's calling to apologize?" Alex asks.

"No, I think he's calling about the sapphire. I never told him that I have it. He's still on a wild goose chase in the U.S. meeting with different dealers, trying to track it down."

"Why didn't you tell him you had it?"

"I suppose I didn't trust him," I admit. "It was a whirl-wind romance after all. And as it turns out, I'm glad I didn't trust him. And in the end, he'll find out from his dad that all is well with the sapphire, and he can go about his merry way romancing my best friend."

Alex just raises one eyebrow at me, and swallows down the rest of the tea, only spilling a little down his chin this time.

Chapter 28

"Being phony is okay if you're honest about it."

"I t's a phony, but I'll take it anyway," Nan would say, whenever a dealer wanted to sell us anything they claimed was vintage, antique, original, or rare. She said this with such authority that it made the dealer instantly bring down the asking price. Nine times out of ten, it was actually a fake, and Nan would argue the price down to something reasonable.

"Why buy it at all if it's a fake?" I once asked her when I was a sulky teenager. I was in a stage where designer clothes seemed to matter at school, and I was embarrassed about wearing the store-brand knock-off clothing, which, let's face it, was all we could afford. All I wanted was one item that I could show off at school. Can we say Adidas, Uggs, or Converse, or hell, just anything not purchased at the Payless Shoe Source? In all my teenage wisdom, I was sure I was the authority on authentic versus fake.

"Because we are not just selling authentic antiques, Gracie, we are selling nostalgia, beauty, and pleasure," Nan responded.

"And dead people's crap," I added in my jaded tone.

"Yes, a little of that, too," Nan sighed. She went on, "In my opinion, if someone wants to put this reproduction of an 1860's washstand in their hallway, and they get pleasure from it, who am I not to sell it to them?"

"You mean you're going to tell them it's the real thing?"

"Heavens, no! I wholeheartedly believe in selling reproductions if they make people happy, but I would never ever lie about them."

"Okay, so fakes are okay, but lies are not okay?"

"In my shop, yes, but let's call them reproductions, shall we? And I write that right on the price tag, so there's no deception."

"Is it lying to call the store Antique Junction then, if they're not all real antiques?" I asked. I could be annoyingly literal sometimes.

"Good point, although I think our customers understand. Have you got a better idea?"

"How about Antique Junk-tion?" I said.

At this Nan burst out laughing. As much as she loved the store, she had to admit that we traded in a lot of outright junk that might be better off for everyone if it were in the landfill already. We were the living embodiment of the expression "one person's trash is another person's treasure."

I've got to give Nan credit. After this conversation, she actually pursued the name change. She thought Antique Junk-tion might just about catch someone's eye and bring us new business. But ultimately she found it too much paperwork to change the name completely, so we just added an "& Etc." to the end of our store sign, even though it kind of makes no sense. And thus our rebirth as Antique Junction & Etc.

"Hatton Garden – where all the finest jewelers are. My ex used to find every excuse to bring me to this street. So on the bright side, I know where the hidden parking spots usually are," Alex says, maneuvering his small car through the heavy London traffic.

I don't see any spaces whatsoever, but sure enough, just when I've given up hope, he spots one. Before I can even get my mind around the physics of parallel parking in a car with the steering wheel on the right side, he backs into a space expertly, leaving only an inch, excuse me, *2.54 centimetres*, to spare. I wait in the car while he finds Benjamin's dad's shop. I don't want anything to do with the handoff of the sapphire. And I certainly don't want to meet Benjamin's father. In my mind, this is an issue between Alex and Benjamin's dad now.

I busy myself with people watching. The people of London are pretty awesome. They dress a touch nicer than New Yorkers, at least here in Hatton Garden, and the blend of influences from Europe, northern Africa, the middle east, and the far east creates a colorful tapestry out the VW Golf window. People seem to be finishing their lunch hours and disappearing into revolving doors where they will go attend to whatever important business occupies their time.

Not five minutes later, Alex gets back in the car with a befuddled look on his face. He's got the necklace in his hand.

"It's a fake," he says quietly.

"Come again?" I say.

"Come again?" he says, looking confused.

"Yea, it means 'what the hell did you just say?'" I say frantically.

"I said it's a fake."

"That's what I thought you said."

I stared at the necklace. If this was fake, then where had Princess Diana's stone gone? Were both Benjamin and his father making up the whole story? And if so, why?

"Why are you saying it's a fake?" I shout at Alex one more time.

"Because that's what the bloody jeweler just told me!"

"The diamonds too?"

"No, they appear to be the original diamonds, but they were not all that valuable."

I take it from his hand and look at it. I feel like a losing contestant on Antiques Roadshow who was just unceremoniously told that the faded poster in Grandma Lily's attic was not in actuality a real Picasso. It occurs to me that I haven't looked at it closely since picking it up at the police station. I've been so nervous about it being stolen or dropping it or in some other way losing it that I haven't spent any time enjoying looking at it. It is a beautiful work of art. Elegant, set perfectly, designed to draw the eye directly toward the center. But the sapphire? I have to admit, it doesn't look as brilliant as I thought it should. Is he right? Is it really a fake?

I need a jeweler's loupe. I need to know.

I open the car door, storm out of the car with the necklace, and into the jewelry store. A frail man with a cap covering his head is behind the counter, his back towards me as he arranges a display.

He turns as I barge in. I recognize the chemo effects instantly – no eyebrows, no eyelashes, slow movements. And I recognize the aquamarine eyes, their radiance magnified by the toll the chemo is taking.

"You must be Grace. I've heard s-so much about you," he says with a slight stutter, and he hands me the loupe without my even asking. When I look through the loupe, I see air bubbles clear as day. It's definitely glass. It's not even artificial lab-created sapphire. It's simply glass.

Alex has followed me into the store and the three of us stare at the necklace.

"I- I'm so sorry," I stammer.

"Excuse me if I'm being thick," Alex says to Benjamin's

father. "But if this is fake, that means the one in the Princess's necklace is real after all, and that you never made the switch, right? Isn't that good news?"

Benjamin's father shakes his head. "I know better than I know myself that the Princess's stone is artificial. As for the real gem, perhaps your mother sold it off at some point. Wouldn't have been a bad idea. Any jeweler would have paid a fortune for it," Benjamin's dad explains. "I've tried to keep my eyes and ears open for it ever since I realized the enormous mistake I made. Usually when a piece that big is on the market, word gets around. But I guess it got out there without me knowing it. I'm going to have to come clean with the Windsor family that the Princess's sapphire is gone. The only thing worse than going down with the stain on my record is keeping up this lie."

"I just don't get it," I say. "When I took it from my mother's safe deposit—"

At that moment, the door swings open, and my jaw drops.

It's Benjamin.

If it's possible, he has gotten better looking since I last saw him. He's carrying a backpack and dragging a suitcase on wheels behind him. He looks like he hasn't slept in days. My emotions are working overtime and my heart is aching, but I try to stand tall.

"Grace! What are you d-doing here?" he says. His stutter has returned.

"It's a long story with a depressing ending," I say, looking at the fake necklace in my hands.

Benjamin glances over at Alex, and I can see him working out the family resemblance in a flash. His eyes bore into me, with a look of hurt I hadn't seen before. It takes my breath away, even though I'm supposed to be the one who is hurt.

"The bigger question is why on earth won't either of you take my bloody calls?" he says, turning to his Dad too.

"It's that damn mobile. My charger has gone missing, and I keep forgetting to do anything about it until the shops are all closed," his father says.

Benjamin reaches into his backpack and pulls out a package wrapped in paper. The three of us turn to stare at him. It cannot be. Or can it? As he begins to unwrap the package, I know he has found it.

The sapphire gleams the way it did when I found it in my mother's safe deposit box. This is how I remember it. There's no mistaking it.

We all gaze at it, dumbstruck.

"Where did you ever –" we all begin speaking at once.

"It's a long story with a depressing ending," Benjamin says, looking at me. He hands the gem to his father, and turns around to leave the building, but his suitcase doesn't make it over the lip of the doorway, and he's struggling to hold the door open and maneouver the suitcase through it.

Alex turns to me with what he must have practiced as an expression of fatherly encouragement and nudges me forward with that chin motion you only see people make in movies. "Go!" he says, under his breath.

I turn up my courage and go to hold the door open for Benjamin.

"Can we at least talk?" he asks.

Chapter 29

"Antique shops, thrift shops – it's all about giving things a second chance."

Nan kept a small set of Hummel figurines in a corner curio cabinet near the back corner of the store. I remember staring at the cherubic face on one of the figurines and trying to make sense of the little elfin boy holding three red-eyed bunny rabbits who seemed to be the fairytale versions of the perfect rabbit, no disrespect to Spike, mind you. The boy had a large round head, rosy cheeks, perfectly almond-shaped eyes, painted lips. Cute, yes. My style? No. It's not that I had anything against Hummel figurines, but I just couldn't imagine what anyone would do with them. I wasn't one for nick-nacks, and to spend hundreds of dollars for a figurine that would only collect dust made no sense to me.

Until I learned a little more about Hummel figurines. First released in the mid 1930's and continuing into the 1940's, the figurines were made by Franz Goebel's porcelain company based on the artwork of a Nun named Maria Hummel. It turns out that Nun Maria Hummel was roundly hated by Adolf Hitler for making the children of Germany look like they had, in his words, "hydrocephalic heads," and the figurines were banned from being sold in Germany during World War II. But here's what's really kickass about this nun. Not cowed by the stinging criticism by the dictator about her *round-headed figurines, she continued to make artwork, including some that portrayed angels wearing gowns with the Star of David as well as one piece with a menorah and a cross, symbolizing the Old and the New Testament together.*

This story gave me a new appreciation for the Hummel figurines indeed. I've now got a small row of Hummel porcelain rabbits lining my windowsill, keeping Spike company. They're still too cute for words, and they do collect a lot of dust, but I'm giving them a second chance. And I think it's worth it.

In the spirit of giving people a second chance, Benjamin and I find a bench about a block from his father's jewelry store, and I let Benjamin explain, or at least I let him start to explain before I interrupt him.

"It was F-F-Felicity," he begins.

"I know, I called you while you were in her bedroom, don't you remember?" I say, still snarky.

"I was never in her b-b-bed, Grace," he says directly.

"That may be just a technicality," I say, still being stubborn.

"How can I get you to listen to what I'm saying? I did not kiss her, touch her, sleep with her, nothing! And I've been trying to t-t-tell you that, but you won't t-t-take my calls."

"That's because I'm hurt. Look, I'm not blind. I know she's prettier than I am and a whole load more fun. I know that guys like you don't go for someone like me. I knew you were too good to be true, but I let you break my heart anyway," I say.

"You've got it all wrong, Grace. Give me five m-m-minutes to explain, and if you don't believe me, then you can leave. D-d-deal?"

"Okay," I say reluctantly.

We sit on a bench along the sidewalk, and he wheels up his suitcase and holds it between his knees.

"It started in New York. You remember the dealer I was m-m-meeting in New York? The one who was selling a 24-carat sapphire? I met him in the showroom in Manhattan, and as soon as I saw the stone, I knew it was the stone my f-f-father had described – the Princess's sapphire. The pattern of inclusions matched up perfectly.

"I made an offer, and right then and there he called the owner on his mobile to confirm the price was acceptable, and I saw the contact information ring up as 'Felicity.' The c-coincidence was too great to ignore. So I asked to meet the owner, which is not standard practice, but I smooth talked my way into it. You Americans really fall for a good British accent," he says.

"You can say that again," I say, and nod for him to continue, the pieces starting to fall into place in my head.

"So we m-met at a pub, and sure enough, it was your Felicity. By the time the dealer and I arrived, Felicity was, what do you call it, three sheets to the wind? She was clearly surprised at seeing me, and knew she had some explaining to do. Her s-solution was to get drunker and drunker, and to flirt with both of us, take selfies, buy us drinks, and act like we were celebrating this big sale, when I of course still had questions. And when you called, she picked up my phone and said whatever drunken thing she said that convinced you we were on a date. The dealer finally left, and Felicity went to the loo, but didn't r-return. It turns out she had passed out. So yes, I took her home that night, the whole way out to Brooklyn in a cab, cost me a fortune, and was waiting for her sister to come home and take care of her," he explains.

"Felicity took the sapphire out of my mother's necklace, so she could sell it?"

"Yes. She told me that she was s-storing it in her safe for you, before you bought your own safe, and in that time, she replaced it with a fake, completely glass, and kept the real stone," Benjamin says.

"So now you know that I lied to you about the necklace, too," I say, feeling worse than a slug under a rock. "I had the necklace – or at least I thought I had it – all along."

"I g-get that. You didn't know me that well. I probably wouldn't have told me either," he says. "But what's k-k-killing me is that you think I would have cheated on you, Grace. Don't you s-s-see?"

I look up at him, wanting so much to believe him, but it still isn't adding up. "What about yesterday when you called me. She was still with you. I heard her voice."

"That's the next thing you n-need to know, Grace. It turns out Felicity is sick. That night when I took her home? When her sister finally arrived, Felicity kind of came out of the drunk and woke up raging. Like a violent rage against her sister, against me. I don't know where the energy came from, but the two of us had to restrain her to the point where Suze called emergency services. Felicity's been in the psych ward for over a week, pretty heavily sedated. They're thinking bipolar d-d-disorder, like her mother has, but it takes a while for those meds to start working. Suze asked me to sit with her that day, since you weren't taking her calls and she had no one else, so that's where I was when I called you y-y-yesterday. I hoped that maybe you would talk to both of us. You need to get back and see her, Grace. When she's alert and things start coming back to her, it's eating her up, what she did to you."

We sit for a few moments together, saying nothing.

"That *was* a long story with a depressing ending," I

say.

"Does it have to be an ending?" he asks me.

He takes my hand in his, and it feels warm and strong, and I realize it's me who owes him an apology.

"Would you give me another beginning?" I ask.

"I could give you a beginning, middle, and happy ending if you'd let me," he says.

"Vomit-inducing, Benj. Try again."

"I'll give you all the new beginnings you can ever dream of?" he tries with that half-smile warming on his lips.

"Nah, kind of meaningless," I critique.

"How about I'll give you a new beginning that's more rocking than the Victorian chaise lounge?"

"Now you're talking!" I say, and we lean in to kiss, the kiss that I've been waiting for all my life.

Chapter 30

"Every girl needs a sister, and she
doesn't have to be related."

As I've explained before, Nan found more than one sister. Nan, Geena, Carla, and another woman Jackie who had died before I had even gotten to know her, were inseparable. They had bonded in their late twenties over their crumbling marriages. They had each other's backs, whether it was emergency babysitting, picking up Tylenol at the store, lending money to make rent, or just plain being there.

Fee is the closest thing I have to a sister, which helps explain how utterly wrecked I was when I thought she had lured Benjamin into her bed. But now I need to go to her, and I make plans for a flight back home for the next day.

Until then, I'm getting ready for what promises to be the most surreal evening of my lifetime. I am meeting my biological sisters and brothers. Benjamin has a knack for knowing what I need and tells me he'll come along to the sibling reunion party if I want him to. And I do. He hasn't slept in 48 hours, but he says he wouldn't miss it for the world if it means a lot to me.

The doorbell on Alex's small cottage rings, and I suddenly feel my heart popping out of my chest. I hadn't realized how nervous I am.

Rob, Alexandria, Isabella, and Jack. They arrive all at the same time. Four adults lined up in the doorstep staring at me.

We are all speechless for a moment.

"Met up at the pub beforehand to talk about our new Yankee sister first. Came as a bit of a surprise to us all, having another sibling," says Jack, the youngest of the crew.

At least I think it is Jack talking. I can hardly keep their names straight. But one thing is clear. The Britton blood must be flush with dominant genes. We all look like each other.

"You're the missing link," Isabella says, hugging me warmly. "I've got Dad's jawline, Rob's got his nose, Jack's got his mouth, and you. You're his eyes. Welcome to the family!"

"Right, Isabella, but that doesn't explain why the rest of you looks like Scarlett Johansson," Alexandria says. And she's right. Isabella is even more stunningly gorgeous in person than she is in the tabloid photos I saw online.

"Inherited from mom, I guess," she says innocently.

I haven't seen any photos of their mother. She must have been a stunner too.

"Not mom's looks, mind you," Alexandria says, turning to me, taking me into confidence. "What she inherited was my mom's natural ability to choose the right surgeon."

Those sound like fighting words to me, but Isabella just laughs.

"If you think about it, Alexandria, we're not so different, are we? You just go for the ink while I go for the

Botox."

Rob and Jack each offer me a hug too. It's a different sensation, to be hugging a brother. It's not warm and fuzzy, like hugging my new half-sisters. But there's a feeling of acceptance that I hadn't expected. And I feel that I don't have to prove myself in any way.

Jack says, "Look at you then. You haven't just got his eyes. You've got his nose, mouth, jaw, and chin. You're a spitting image! But a lot nicer looking than dad!"

"And hey!" Rob says, as we break our embrace. "I'm no longer a club of one! No longer alone in the world," he says, with a melodramatic back of his hand draped on his forehead.

"And what exactly are the club's membership benefits?" I ask.

"Well, I'm glad you asked. You see, it's a little known fact that illegitimacy in the Britton family has its privileges."

"And they are?"

"Invisibility, incorruptibility, and insignificance."

"Sounds *in*viting," I say.

"How about *in*corrigible?" Jack says, elbowing Rob in the ribs.

I turn to introduce my new family to Benjamin, but he's disappeared.

"Don't just stand in the doorway! Make yourselves at home," Alex says as he gathers everyone's coats and brings them to the upstairs bedroom.

We head to the living room, only to find Benjamin sitting in the corner of the sofa, head tilted back and snoring like a jackhammer. He doesn't move a muscle when we all sit down around him. I shake him a little. No response, just more snores.

His snores begin to take on the character of the conversation, punctuating our stories and filling up the awkward pauses. I sense my siblings warming up to him, even though he's sacked out.

"Selfie time!" Alexandria shrieks, and we all pile around Benjamin, mugging for the camera, with him in the center, completely oblivious to the fun he is missing.

With seven empty bottles of wine and the detritus from a takeaway curry littering Alex's kitchen, laughter is filling the small house. And I've learned an important lesson. You can't really believe what you read about the nobility on the internet. Yes, my new siblings have had their share of newsworthy screw-ups, but that's only tabloid fodder. They've got careers, hopes, and dreams like the rest of us.

I've never felt so welcome anywhere as I do tonight.

But Benjamin is right. I need to get back home to see what I can do to help Felicity.

Chapter 31

"Don't sweat the small change."

When I was a teenager, Nan had a way of keeping my worries in perspective without belittling them. "Don't sweat the small change," she would say, whenever I was angry or frustrated about a perceived slight or a bad grade or a bad hair day. "Save your worries for the big bucks." One of the few places you could sweat the small change was right in front of our store. We had a 1960's era bubblegum machine, a Ford floor model with a cast iron base and a turnkey that still worked. As a young girl, it was one of my jobs to keep it filled with bubble gumballs. Nan used to be able to find the authentic gumballs with the word Ford printed on them, but over the years, we had to settle for Dubble Bubble or whatever brand was available.

Every morning I would roll the gumball machine on its base to the spot outside the store next to our sidewalk sign. Groups of elementary school students would take detours home from school just to buy a gumball. We always kept a stash of dimes available for kids who didn't have any change, and as soon as the change receptacle filled up, we'd recycle the dimes for the next swarm of children.

What little profit we would make from the gumball machines was given to charity, the way the original Ford Gum company founder Ford Mason would have liked it. He was the first vending machine company to intermingle business *and charity in this way, selling the machines to charities, who would set the machines up in highly trafficked places, where Ford would deliver the gumballs and share the profits with the charities.*

I remember feeling dejected when the Ford gumball machine sold, but Nan was quick to barter a good deal on another one, and since then, I haven't sold a gumball machine without having another one as a backup.

I fly into JFK. Felicity has been released from the hospital and is still staying with Suze in Brooklyn. She looks like her usual beautiful self when I go in to hug her, and she embraces me for what must be a full minute. Maybe two.

"I've missed you, Fee."

"I owe you many apologies. I don't even know where to begin," she says.

Do you forgive your BFF for stealing from you? Do you forgive your BFF for throwing herself at your boyfriend? And even if you do, do you ever trust her in the same way? This isn't the same "small change" Nan was talking about. I wasn't sure I could brush it under the carpet.

But I study her face. When I look at her more closely, I notice her eyes look older. The twinkles have faded. She looks so serious and sad. Her diagnosis has shaken her, and it's breaking my heart. I find myself hoping the old Felicity isn't lost.

"Aw c'mon Fee. I know that wasn't the real Felicity," I say. And we hug again, and I feel that maybe I can forgive her. A surge of lightness and happiness overcomes me, with the weight of our estrangement being lifted.

I agree to stay with Fee while Suze goes to work. Geena is still planning to watch the store for the rest of the week, so I've got the time.

How do we fill the week? First we bond, we bitch, we bake, we binge watch.

She goes for the romantic comedies. Me? I still go for the retro. A good sit-com from the 1970's or 1980's is perfect for lambasting to pieces. Some of them are so bad, they're good. Honestly, did no one think *I Dream of Jeannie* was even just a smidgen sexist back then? For god's sake, she spent the entire show waltzing around in a bikini for her master. The Brady Bunch? Now, I love kitsch as much as the next Hulu streamer, but was there ever any whiter family than the Bradies? We watch a few episodes of Facts of Life, to rave over the 80's hairstyles, which are epically large and endlessly fascinating to me.

Of all of them, I think Taxi stands the test of time more than the others. We actually start getting into the plotline of Alex, Bobbie, Louie and the rest. We like the way everyone's got issues, but no one's taking anything too seriously.

Next we ponder, we prattle, we plan, we plot.

Fee loves New York, and Suze wants to keep her nearby, to help her monitor her moods and get her meds working. What better place for a jeweler to make a go of it? And she's got a free sofa to sleep on until she gets back on her feet.

"I feel like the worst BFF already, and on top of that, now I'm leaving you high and dry in New Jersey," Fee says, sadly.

And she's right. The prospect of spending day after day in *Antique Junction & Etc.* without Fee's daily lunch breaks isn't exactly tantalizing. I love the gang there, but I don't want to turn into an antique myself.

And of course, there's Benjamin. And my new British family. Nan told me never to trust anything that's shiny and new. But that's the thing about them. They may be new to me, but there's something about them that feels like I've known them all my life, as trite as that may sound.

I think about Geena, Carla, and Jakob. My found family. Each one of them has supported me as long as I can remember.

"They love you like family, Grace," Fee says. "They'll still be there for you, wherever you are. If I know Geena, she will physically stick you on that plane to England if it means you'd be happier. That's all she wants for you. And Carla? She's a live-in-the-moment kind of woman. She might even join you if that dude Ian ever decides to put out," Fee laughs.

It's good to hear her laughing again.

No sooner do we utter Carla's name than my mobile lights up with her number.

"Hang on to your hat, Grace, I've got news!"

"News? Is everything okay?" I ask.

"Yes, your Spike has been one busy boy!"

"Is he driving you crazy?"

"First off, no, I love him."

"Me too. Give him kisses for me. Second?"

"Second, he just gave birth to 8 baby bunnies."

Silence.

More silence.

"Um, do you think we should re-name him?"

Chapter 32

*"Travel may be expensive, but a new
perspective is priceless."*

One of the fastest moving items at our store that's
hardest to keep in stock is the Art Deco travel
posters. I keep a stock of reproductions of these
posters, but the originals are hard to come by. The early posters, say from the 1920s, were commissioned by rail lines,
and they evoke an earlier, simpler time, like a slice of history
hanging on your living room wall.

Later the airlines commissioned them too, often hiring
famous artists and illustrators to design them. The vibrant
colors, stylized figures, and the sanitized view of these major
travel destinations are pleasant to the eye, and appeal to our
handful of younger customers. And by younger, well, I don't
actually mean younger. It's usually empty nesters in their
late 50's or early 60's who are setting up a downsized version
of life and looking for inspiration for their walls.

"Photography has destroyed the glamour of travel," Nan
said once, "But fix this poster in my mind's eye, and I'm a
happy traveler," she continued, admiring a new vintage-look-
alike poster that had come in. It depicted Detroit with a glam-
orous flapper stepping out into the light, the Detroit skyline
gleaming in the background, and the tremendous metallic
sheen of the Lincoln's fender casting a glow on the flapper's
perfect skin, as her elegant outstretched finger brushes over

the headlight. Motor City had had its share of downturns since those days, but even still, it was hard to imagine any city ever looking that sparkly. But we can always dream.

Sparkle, nee Spike, turns out to be a terrific mom. He's endlessly patient as his babies are nursing. He eats and sleeps whenever they're not nursing, and I miss him snuggling with me. His babies are not what I would call cute. But I know they will be some day, and I start lining people up to adopt them. Thanks to the wonders of modern social media, I have seven of them placed within the first week.

The issue is Carla. She has fallen into true love with the rabbit formerly known as Spike. She stops by every afternoon at closing time to check in on Spike. She refers to the babies as her grandbunnies. She brings a fresh head of lettuce every day, and my fridge is overflowing to the point where I have to take drastic action. I start eating salads myself. And I have to admit, they aren't all that bad.

I've spent the weekend and this morning with Geena and Jakob in the store. We are moving everything out of the main show room and squeezing it into the back display areas, because the renovation crew is coming first thing tomorrow morning.

As much as I love rearranging things, rearranging can only go so far. It's like putting on makeup when what you really need is a facelift. I am ecstatic that a real professional renovation is finally going to happen. I'm finally going to have the shelving, lighting, and flooring that Nan had always dreamed of. I only wish she were here to see it.

I'm back upstairs in my apartment when Carla stops by yet again, with a new kind of lettuce for Spike and the babies. Radicchio. She's going gourmet on me.

"Radicchio! You think he'll like it? I've never seen him eat anything purple."

"I don't think he'll mind the color. In fact, rabbits aren't able to see much color at all," Carla says, lecturing me like a teacher.

"You been studying?" I say.

"Yes, I want to be a good rabbit mom when one of these kittens is ready to come home with me," Carla says. This from a woman who admits that she hates it when human babies come into her coffee shop.

"Aw, look, Spike looks happy to see you." And sure enough, Spike gets up from his bedding and scampers over to see Carla.

"You look terrific, Grace. The flowers are gorgeous. What's the occasion?"

"They just arrived this morning. From Benjamin. He's been sending me fresh flowers once a week! He's got me totally spoiled."

"He's a keeper," Carla says.

"Unlike Ian?" I tease.

"I don't know what overcame me with Ian that day. I found a nice Jersey man. Divorced, three grown children, no major baggage. He even helps out at the coffee shop. He's got a bad back, so I still do all the heavy lifting, but it's still nice to have him around. But you still haven't answered why you're dressed like a million bucks."

"Well, I've got good news and fun news," I say. "The good news is that Benjamin's father is feeling a little better after his last round of chemo. And the fun news is that Benjamin is coming to visit for the rest of the week. His flight is landing in about two hours, and I'm going to pick him up, while Geena watches the store. Does this outfit look okay?"

"If it looked any more okay, I don't think they'd let you step foot in the airport," Carla reassures me.

Another knock at the door. This time, Geena and Jakob together. Jakob closes my front door behind him and throws the bolt lock.

"We're calling an emergency meeting," Geena says.

"Oh no, what's going on?" I immediately assume something terrible has happened in the store.

"You're the emergency!" Geena says.

"Me?"

"Yes, Jakob and I have decided enough is enough. We're staging a coup of the store. You are taking the rest of the week off to be with Benjamin."

"Aw, that's sweet, but the contractors are coming tomorrow."

"You think I can't handle a coupla carpenters?" Jakob says. It's true, there's no one more meticulous about carpentry work than Jakob.

"And after the coup? Our work still isn't finished," Geena says.

She hands me an envelope. Inside is tri-folded printout.

"We're extraditing you," she says.

The printout is a boarding pass for a flight to London, the same day Benjamin is returning. I'm touched, but I'm still worried about leaving the store, Spike's babies, my apartment.

"This is too generous!" I protest.

"Not that generous," Jakob says with a wink. "It's only a one-way ticket."

"The perfect moment to leave will never come if you don't let it. There will always be something going on at the store, some reason that you feel tied to your life here. But don't you see that Benjamin needs you now? His father's sick, and he's trying to run the business and keep up the care for his father at the same time. Couldn't you have used someone when your mom was sick?" Geena says.

I nod. Benjamin is so self-sufficient that I haven't given it enough thought. He's going through exactly what I went through. And even if he doesn't say he needs me there, I know it could mean a lot to him. And isn't that what relationships are all about?

"And you've got 31 years of catching up to do with your family. That's not going to happen if you don't make it happen. Time's a wasting!" Carla chimes in.

So it's decided.

Chapter 33

"Don't spoil the ending by telling me it's the end."

Truth be told, Nan had wanted me to sell the store when she died. She believed there was more to see in the world than the inside of a dingy antique shop. She wanted me to take the proceeds and take a round-the-world trip.

But what she didn't realize was that, like her, I had come to fall in love with *Antique Junction & Etc.* too. She may have opened the store, but I was a part of its history too. I liked carrying on Nan's work. I liked being steeped in the memories of an earlier time during the workday and heading up to my modern apartment upstairs every evening. I liked chit-chatting with the elderly customers inside the store and greeting the school children at the gumball machine in mid-afternoon. I liked decorating the store for the change of seasons and the holidays. I liked being part of the small downtown business-owners' association. I liked planning the store's renovation and envisioning what it could become.

But for the first time, I'm starting to wonder if Nan wasn't right again. It may be time to see the world. It might be time to see if there is something worth keeping between me and Benjamin. And thanks to the generous bonus that Benjamin's dad had insisted on for returning the sapphire, I might not have to choose between the two.

At least not right away.

∞ ∞ ∞

I look at Benjamin from a distance as he's coming through Customs. He hasn't seen me yet, and I try to observe him objectively. He looks tired. He looks kind. He looks responsible. He looks generous. And of course, he looks hot. And I don't mean temperature hot.

"How do you do it, Grace?" is the first thing he says to me.

"Do what?"

"You know, get more and more amazing every time I see you?"

He kisses me lightly and then holds my hand, leading me over to a corner that's not overrun by travelers.

His aquamarine eyes have a translucence that hypnotizes me. He brushes his fingers along my cheek, and under my jaw, and his eyes are seeking something deeper in me. My eyes are a deep brown, nearly black, and I worry he won't find what he is looking for.

His kiss lights me up like I've never been kissed before. He has a way of exploring my lips with his lips that's so tender and so strong at the same time. I'm finally starting to believe that he really does want me for who I am and for how I am. Our kiss is getting deeper. I can feel every nerve ending in my body coming to life, and I'm vaguely aware that we're beginning to attract stares. And I swear someone even has the nerve to take a picture of us. Doesn't anyone have any respect for privacy anymore?

A steely-looking security officer appears to our left.

"Keep it G-rated, or move along," she says.

Benjamin looks up, bewildered that someone would interrupt us.

"Americans can be such prudes," he mutters to me.

Carla may be right about getting kicked out of the airport after all.

∞∞∞

We don't make it anywhere near my Brimnes bed. In fact I'm not sure we make it past the entryway, if my apartment were even big enough to have an entryway. My hands are in his hair, under his shirt, unbuttoning, unlocking, unleashing, as he is trying to set his luggage down, all the while kissing him, and decidedly not in the G-rated fashion.

"No fair taking advantage of a man while his hands are full," he says, as he kicks the door shut behind us.

All the promises we have made during our nightly calls are becoming a reality. Now is the time to fulfill each and every one of them. And I do, and he does. The evening stretches into nighttime in a delicious blur of time and space and bodies.

"That's brilliant, Gracie! You'd really try living in London for a while?"

I tell him about my one-way ticket, the coup of my store, my forced extradition to London, and my plans to get to know my siblings.

"It's lovely. And I'm telling you, the storefronts in Hatton Garden would be perfect for an antique shop, if you ever want to get one going in London. You've got the knowledge and the perfect eye for creating a store that brings people in."

"One step at a time," I say. "It's just an extended visit. You know, exploratory."

He looks a little pensive, and I'm worried that maybe his offer wasn't good anymore. Or that he'd never expected me to say yes. Or — the fear that I still can't seem to shake, despite everything he's told me — that he has a London girlfriend that I don't know about.

"I only wish you'd have told me sooner," he says.

"I don't have to come right now, if you don't want," I say, backing down quickly, knowing it was too good to be true.

"No no! It's just my flat. It's kind of a wreck. I'd have cleaned it for you if I had known!"

"You're talking to a junk store expert. I think I can handle a little mess," I say, relieved.

"I just want you to know that it's not reflective of my usual housekeeping prowess."

"You've got prowess in the housekeeping department too?"

"My prowess is legendary. You've only seen the tip of the iceberg," he says, disappearing beneath the sheets to work his magic again.

∞ ∞ ∞

The week rushes by in a flurry of saying my temporary goodbyes to Geena, Jakob, Carla, and some of my favorite customers.

The construction has started, and I can already tell it's going to be perfect. Jakob is checking that every corner is square and every seam is flush.

Carla is still gaga over Spike and the babies. I've transferred all the bedding, foods, and blankets to her place. She put her loveseat in storage to make way for Spike's family, and I'm starting to doubt whether she will be able to adopt the little ones away to their promised families. She's bonded to each and every one of them, and seems to be able to tell them apart, which is more than I can say, especially considering that I didn't even know Spike was female.

∞∞∞

On our last day, I'm packed and ready for the airport. And it feels so right. Benjamin is upstairs showering, so I stop in the store one last time, take a look at the back rooms, and say goodbye to some of the items that I've grown attached to, that could be gone when I come back.

I'm walking through the section of kitchen dishes and bowls when I hear someone enter the back showroom. It's Benjamin, and I can smell the pleasant scent of his shampoo and aftershave.

"We've got some fond memories in this room, haven't we?" Benjamin says, nodding toward the Victorian chaise across the room. The afternoon light from the rear window is casting a glow behind him, and he looks like he's walking right out of a movie set

I back up into the row of shelves to get a better look at him, his hair still damp and curled at the edges a little. Sometimes I still can't believe that he is real.

He steps toward me, his hands out, and I hold them as he leans down to kiss me again. He has a way of taking me from zero to sixty in about four seconds, and I wonder if we have time for the Victorian chaise again. I start to inch him in that direction, but he must not realize what I'm doing, and before I know what's happening, he pushes back toward me. I lose my balance and start tipping backwards. He reaches out to grab me behind my back, but it is too late, and we're both going down, down to the floor, the momentum unstoppable. He takes one more step forward in a desperate attempt to rescue us both, but his shoulder takes out the corner of the shelf, and in what feels like slow motion, the shelf begins to tip.

"Nooo!" I cry out.

Like a set of larger-than-life dominoes, three shelves keel over in a din of breaking saucers, plates, mugs, and bowls. Shards of rainbow-colored ceramics litter the floor, and after a moment of chaos, the room grows utterly quiet.

Benjamin is unhurt but looks horrified at what we have done.

But me? I laugh. I rejoice. I give Benjamin a huge smooch and thank him for solving my most irritating problem.

My everlasting, dust-collecting, shelf-hogging, heavy-as-shit Fiestaware is finally at rest. And it went out in the blaze of lust and love and radioactive glory that it so deserves. Could there be any better happily ever after?

About The Author

Wendy Coffman

Wendy Coffman loves to read and write fiction to take a break from reality and escape into new places. Her characters and settings have a story to tell, and she hopes her words bring them to life for her readers. Wendy lives in New Jersey with her husband, two children, and a cat named Sam.

Made in the USA
Middletown, DE
09 December 2021

54844344R00136